Changeling Press. LLC

Razor's Edge Press
A Changeling Press LLC Imprint

Monsters In My Closet
Razor's Edge Monster Erotica
Wanda Violet O.

Happy Reachy!

Wanda

"Teika"

Monsters In My Closet
Razor's Edge Monster Erotica
Wanda Violet O.

All rights reserved.
Copyright ©2024 Wanda Violet O.

ISBN: 978-1-60521-896-0

Publisher:
Razor's Edge Press
A Changeling Press LLC Imprint
315 N. Centre St.
Martinsburg, WV 25404
ChangelingPress.com

Printed in the U.S.A.

Editor: Margaret Riley
Cover Artist: Marteeka Karland

Table of Contents

Claimed By The Monster In My Closet (Monster World 1)
A Razor's Edge Monster Erotica Short
By Wanda Violet O.

Believing there's a monster in my closet and dreaming about him masturbating over me are two completely different things. One means I might be crazy. The other? Well. It makes me horny. Imagine my surprise when dreams turn to reality and I'm *claimed* by the *monster in my closet.*

WARNING: This is a short erotica novella... if you want a strong plot and character development, you won't find them here. What you *will* find is hot sex and one satisfied woman -- with a monster out of the closet, and in her bed.

Chapter One

There's a monster in my closet.

No. Really. He's been there since I was a little girl. I never saw anything other than his yellow, glowing eyes until my twentieth birthday. Practically every night after that, he'd wait until I was almost asleep, then the door to my closet would creak open and I'd see him standing there.

He's tall. *Really* tall. And big. Muscles ripple under the fir covering his body. If I stood next to him, the top of my head might come up to his chest. He has the face of a man, but his mouth and nose are slightly wolven. Like he might be a werewolf? I don't know. All I know is I'm equal parts terrified of him and aroused by him.

As my twenty-first birthday neared, he got more aggressive. I could actually hear him snarling when I was in that twilight between sleep and wakefulness. Every time he did that I woke up, my heart pounding, terrified he was going to kill me.

Then two days before my birthday, I looked up to find him standing right beside my bed, snarling and growling. It was a dream. Had to be a dream. This was usually where I woke up, but I couldn't seem to make myself. I was caught in some kind of dream world, unable to break free. The monster in my closet loomed over me. But this time, he gripped his enormous cock in one hand and stroked himself as he looked down at me.

I wanted to scream. I wanted to run away. I wanted...

To reach out and touch it…

Or lick it…

NO! No way. He was a beast! A monster who would likely eat me for supper!

He grunted when I met his gaze, those luminous yellow eyes staring back at me. I tried to roll to the other side of the bed, but his free hand landed heavily on my naked chest. His fist pumped faster, and he roughly squeezed my small breast. I cried out, and he gave a satisfied sounding chuff.

Whimpering in equal parts fear and, surprisingly, budding arousal, I lay passively beneath his hand, afraid to move, afraid of what he might do if I didn't stay still. His breathing became more and more erratic, and he snarled repeatedly, his hand flying up and down his cock. I could see the pearly drops of pre-cum leaking from the tip. Several drops shook loose, only to evaporate in a puff of smoke when they were flung into the air.

Then, with a roar loud enough to make me cover my ears, he threw back his head. A powerful jet of white cum erupted from his cock, turning to smoke seconds after leaving his body. Had it not, he would have lashed my skin with it. My tits. My belly. Maybe my face. Perversely, I found myself opening my mouth and sticking out my tongue as if to catch the ribbons of cum he should have coated me with.

I was horrified by my behavior. How could I openly welcome him? Could I really be turned on by the monster in my closet? Could I really want his cum in my mouth? Or his cock down my throat?

No. This was nothing more than a nightmare,

and I was caught in some kind of dreamscape where I was acting out of character. Had to be. There was no way I truly wanted something like that.

Was there?

Once his breathing had returned to normal, his body faded. Just before he disappeared, and I was once more fully awake, his voice came to me as he stared into my eyes.

"One more night, human. One more night and then... *You're mine.*" He grinned, trailing a hand down my body to rest lightly on top of my mound. "I suggest you get rid of your virginity before then. Otherwise, your first night might start out less than desirable."

Then I was awake, the wild scent of woods and earth surrounding me like he was still standing over me. I shivered, soaked in sweat, the air conditioning too cool on my damp skin.

One more night...

What did that mean? And how was I supposed to get rid of my virginity before then? I didn't have any hook up prospects. Was it just the lingering effects of sleep that made me dream those last words? I thought I was awake, but maybe I was still fighting to wake up. I hoped so. Because, if not, the monster in my closet was real. And he was coming for me on the night of my twenty-first birthday. And sex was definitely on his mind.

* * *

I didn't dream any more after that. Not that night or the next. I'd all but forgotten the mixture of fear and erotic excitement with the celebration that followed. My friends and I went to a concert and drank way too much. Illegal? Yeah. But you only turn twenty-one once and I was determined to push my boundaries. And for some reason, the longer the night went on, the more I thought about the strange dream I'd had. Which just made me horny.

I thought about what the monster's last words to me. *One more night and then... You're mine.* Then there was that suggestion I get rid of my virginity. Yeah. Not helping my current drunken, horny state.

I looked around me. We'd gone to a dance club for my party. Fake IDs all around. Yea! There had been a couple of guys hitting on me throughout the night, but I didn't want to fuck some strange guy. At least, not all the way. But maybe I could talk one of them into taking my virginity without actually fucking me.

The more I thought about it, the better my intoxicated brain liked the idea. Which begged the question. Was I actually preparing myself for the monster tonight? And did I really want to get rid of my virginity this way? With a stranger? Without sex even? Because I *really* wanted sex.

Fuck it. If the monster didn't like it, he shouldn't have told me to get rid of it. I wasn't buying a sex toy because it was damned embarrassing and my parents would intercept any package I got in the mail. So fucking a stranger it was. Because yeah. No way I'm fucking a boy I know and have it get out I'll fuck anything that moves.

I was sitting at the bar trying to decide which guy to make my play for when a wide shouldered, dark-headed man sat next to me with a faint grin.

"May I buy you a drink, love?" His accent was some kind of English derivative, but not quite. Then again, I was drunk. All I know for sure was it sounded sexy as fuck.

"Absolutely."

He motioned to the bartender. "Whatever the lady wants."

When the bartender looked at me, I held up my glass, which was mostly ice now. "Captain and Coke." He smiled and filled my request.

I took a healthy swig and sighed as the euphoria I was currently in got another kick. "Mmmm," I said, savoring the bittersweet concoction. "My favorite."

"Bit of a pirate, are you?"

I grinned at him. "If I say yes, will you make me shiver my timbers?"

We both laughed.

"Got a name?" I asked.

"Daemon," he said, his grin a little sinister, but not unpleasant.

"Well, Daemon, I'm Wyn." I stuck out my hand. "Pleased to meet you."

He took my hand with a little chuckle. "Well, lovely Wyn. What is it you want? Hmmm?"

The alcohol had hit me just right. I had a loose tongue and didn't care a bit to tell this stranger what I needed from him. "I have a little problem," I confessed, leaning close so I could talk to him over the pounding of the music. "I turned twenty-one today. Don't tell the bartender because I gave him a fake ID."

Damon chuckled at my ear, brushing it with

his mouth. "Your secret is most assuredly safe with me, little Wyn. Is that all you have to confess?"

"No," I said. "I'm a virgin, and I need not to be?"

He nuzzled my neck with his lips this time, his laughter deep and warm. I thought I felt his tongue dart out to taste my skin, but I wasn't sure. "Need? That's an odd way to phrase it, don't you think?"

"Well," I said, raising my hand to smooth his crisp, dark shirt over his shoulder then over his chest. The muscles playing under my palm made me shiver with desire. "This is going to sound crazy, but there's a monster in my closet. And he's coming for me tonight."

"I see. If he's coming for you, wouldn't he want you to be untouched when he takes your little body?"

I shrugged, his words an unexpected turn on. Probably the alcohol. "He said I needed to get rid of it or I might not have as pleasant a time. I don't own any toys and don't have time to get one tonight, so I'm going to need you to fuck me."

Instead of laughing at me or leaving me because I was either crazy or too drunk to make sound decisions, he nodded his head solemnly. "I understand." He stood and held out his hand. "Come with me, sweet. Let's see what we can do to get you ready for the big evening ahead."

I wasn't sure what I was expecting, but Daemon took me to the dance floor. At first, I was annoyed. I thought I'd made myself clear what I wanted, and he took me dancing? What the fuck? But then he pulled me close to him, his very hard, very impressive erection pressing against my belly as he moved with me. I gasped, clinging to him. When I looked up at him, his gaze was hot and filled with lust.

I slid my arms around his neck and put my lips to his ear. "I thought you were going to fuck me?"

"Oh, we'll get there, *muluk alhayawanat al'alifa.* But you'll be so fucking wet it will make your breaching much easier. And the easier it is on you, the more pleasure for me."

My knees went weak and my skin erupted in goose bumps. He noticed my reaction and tightened his hold on me as he took my earlobe in his mouth and nibbled gently.

I have no idea how long we danced, but it didn't take long for me to lose my inhibitions. I wasn't doing anything anyone else wasn't doing, but it was the first time I'd ever let a man grind on me. Or touch my breasts. I'd had a boy or two cop a feel of my ass before, but, though I hadn't discouraged it, I never let it go any further. Tonight, I was going way further. All the way further. This man currently cupping my tits as I ground my ass against his dick was going to fuck me. Take my virginity. *And I was starving for it*!

As we moved around the floor, I noticed other couples in various stages of foreplay. One guy had his hand inside a girl's top while she arched to his touch. I saw one of my girlfriends in the embrace of a very large man with another man at her back. She kissed the man at her back over her shoulder, while the other dipped his head and sucked on one nipple he'd pulled out of her slinky dress. Another woman

I didn't know had her leg over her partner's hip while his hand was under her skirt. Judging by the look on her face, he probably had his fingers in her pussy.

"You enjoy watching?"

"One of those girls is my friend," I said inanely. "That's so fucking hot."

"Ah, you do like watching. Don't worry. You'll love the experience even more." He wound one arm around my waist and the other over my breasts. "Feel the heat of my skin through your dress," he said at my ear. "I can feel your little nipples stabbing my arm. I bet they're lush and sweet. Like ripe berries."

"Touch them," I whimpered. "Do like that man's doing to my friend and suck on one."

"Oh, no, little pet. That's not for me. Your virginity is. It's what you've gifted me with and I intend to take it. The only question is how you want me to take it."

"I..." I looked back at him. "What do you mean?"

His smile remained equal parts sexy and sinister. This time, I thought he was having very dirty thoughts and I just had to hear them. "Well, we can go to a room and I can seduce you nicely, or..."

My belly fluttered at the promise of something naughty and decadent. Something forbidden. "Or what?"

"Or I can take you here in the middle of the crowd."

Chapter Two

"OhmyGod! That's so fuckin *hot*!" People were mashed up against us on the floor, sweating, writhing bodies all needing sex as hard as I needed it. Daemon was offering to give me what everyone else wanted but were too big of a pussy to take. At least, that's what my alcohol befuddled mind was telling me. Whatever. It *did* sound fucking hot. "What if it hurts too much to do it here?"

"I suppose you'll have to trust me to ease you through it. But if it hurts, we can stop and finish somewhere else. I think you can take me though." He gave me a satisfied smirk, as if just by answering him the way I had proved some point I'd missed.

"You'd do that? Take my virginity. Fuck me in front of everyone?"

"Sweet pet. If you're correct, you're about to be fucked by the monster in your closet. What is this compared to that?"

"Good point." I shivered in excitement. "We'd do it here?"

He slid his palm up my thigh under my short dress to my hip. I didn't know how badly he'd exposed me and didn't much care. "Oh, yes, sweet pet. I'll do that. If you're good, I might put my cum in your little pussy for the monsters to taste. That way they'll know you've had your virginity taken by fucking and will know you can take all they have to give. Would you let me do that?"

"Come inside me? Are you crazy?" Hell no, he couldn't come inside me! What the fuck? Except, my pussy spasmed and I was pretty sure I came a little at the thought.

He nipped my neck with his teeth sharply even as he laughed softly. "No more crazy than you are, shall we say."

Well, I had told him about the monster in my closet. The one promising to fuck me tonight. The one who wanted me to get rid of my virginity before he came to me.

"Good point. You think he'd like what you said? To know I'd been fucked instead of taking it myself?"

"If the monster needs your innocence removed badly enough to not take it himself, then yes. He'll want to know you're ready to take a big cock. Maybe more than one big cock?"

I thought for a moment while Daemon's hand slid in front of my body to pet my bare mound lazily. "He didn't say anything about more than one."

"In my culture, monsters run in packs. Several would control a realm. I bet the one who will take you tonight will be the leader of their clan. He'll claim you for himself, but his brothers will get their share as well."

"Are you making fun of me?" If he was, that was the end of this. Fucker.

"Oh, no, pretty little pet. I'm being deadly serious." The look on his face said he was. "You need to be prepared not only physically, but mentally. If your monster is truly coming for you, you need to know what will happen."

"Multiple monsters?"

"Four at least. Maybe five or six."

"Oh. My. God."

"Pet, God has little to do with this situation. This is strictly the stuff of nightmares."

"Will they hurt me?" I was starting to really believe this guy -- the whole situation, really -- when I'd almost convinced myself I just had an overactive imagination and had a nightmare.

"If they intended that, sweet pet, they'd never have suggested you lose your virginity. They'd want to hurt you in that way. Only a select few monsters enjoy that kind of thing, and they are never given virgins."

Before I could contemplate that, Daemon's fingers slid under my panties and over my mound to my clit. I broke out in a sweat.

"Your little pussy is creaming nicely. You really are a hot little piece, aren't you." He didn't seem to expect me to respond so I didn't. Not sure I could have if I'd wanted to. "So soft and wet. So fucking perfect for the masters." Not sure what he meant by that, but I was beyond caring.

Daemon turned me around, ripping my panties from my hips and pulling the front of my dress above my bald little pussy. He looked down into my eyes and grinned. "Take out my cock, pet. Don't unbutton my fly, just unzip me." I did as he instructed. He kept us close so that the folds of my skirt at least partially covered him. "Now, sweet pet, tuck my cock between your legs and let me swim in the wetness I coaxed from you."

I did. When he pulled me tighter to him and gave a little thrust at the same time, his cock slid through my wet pussy lips like silk. If he hadn't been holding me up, I would have crumpled to the floor because my knees just buckled. I whimpered and he chuckled as he adjusted his grip on my body.

"Steady, sweet pet. There's much more to come and much more for you to endure." He cocked his head to the side. "I wonder If I can make you come on your first fuck?"

My head spun with a combination of the alcohol and the situation. I was certain I was hyperventilating. I gripped his shoulders weakly and let my head fall forward to his chest.

"You're going to fuck me standing up? Right here?"

"Oh yes. Feel my dick between your luscious lips?"

"Yes!"

"Now." He adjusted himself just that little bit. "Feel the head of my cock at your entrance."

My gaze snapped to his. "I do."

With Daemon looking into my eyes, I stood still as he fed his cock into my weeping cunt one slow inch at a time while we stood on the dance floor with bodies grinding against us and each other in a hedonistic dance. It felt like a pagan ritual to me and I was the virgin sacrifice. There was a sharp pinch, then he was as far in as he could get.

Daemon reached between us then brought his hand up to inspect the blood staining his fingers. The second he did, the lights on the dance floor strobed. Or maybe it was just my lust filled brain. I glanced at Daemon and his eyes seemed to glow under the black lights under the strobe. I was mesmerized by the flashing lights and the intensity of his gaze.

He dipped his hand back to our joined bodies and rubbed all around my opening, around his cock, then brought his fingers back between us. More blood. This time, one small drop dripped between us, landing on the front of my skirt.

"It's done," he said. "Now. I'm going to make you come. When you do, you're going to milk my cum from me into your tight little pussy. You're no longer the virgin sacrifice, pretty pet. You're now ready for the monsters to take you. They will be brutal, but they will care for you as long as you don't fight them. Resist, and they may not see to your pleasure."

Resist? Who could resist? I was horny as a motherfucker and he was talking about resisting? "Make me come, Daemon," I whispered. Somehow, I knew he heard me, even over the raging music. "I want to scream when I do."

"Scream away, my dear. You'll draw a crowd and others might feel the need to fuck you as well."

"Others?"

"Oh yes. As there are strong clans of monsters, there are many of us who serve them. If you're freshly fucked by several of us, we'll be handsomely rewarded."

"They'd want more than one person to fuck me? He seemed pretty possessive. Are you sure?"

"Sweet pet, they are much, much bigger than us. Their cocks would rend a virgin in two. The more used to fucking you are, the more likely you are to come away undamaged."

That was comforting. *Not!* "Wait. You serve the monster in my closet?" I could just make out a second visage for Daemon. When the strobes cast shadows, there seemed to be another side of Daemon that was hidden. And he was decidedly demonic.

"Oh yes, pet. Do you think they would send just anyone to take your innocence? You're to be protected -- and pleasured -- any time you're in this realm. They have no desire to cause you distress. My advice?" He grinned. "Just roll with it."

Who was I to argue?

Damon began to move inside me. At first, it was a slow, steady roll. Just a lazy glide, as if he were still trying to conceal that we were actually fucking on the dance floor. The strobes still flashed, creating that illusion of jerky movement all around us. It was surreal. Like everyone around us were puppets and had no clear notion of anything outside their little bubble.

One by one, we were joined by other men. They all had women they danced with, but the women didn't seem to realize anything unusual was going on. The men pulled their partners close, grinding on them much like Daemon did me only I'm fairly certain they all had their dicks in their pants. Until one moved in behind me.

"We've heard about you for years," he said, cupping my breasts through my dress. His cock was mashed against my ass as he held me still for Daemon's thrusts. "We managed to keep away any male who might take your virginity. Had we not, we wouldn't have gotten to have this night with you."

Then I felt his cock slid between my ass cheeks and nestle in my crack. He moved up and down, fucking between my cheeks while Daemon continued his sensual rhythm in and out of my cunt.

"Steady," the man said at my ear. "I'm going to ease inside you…"

Ease inside me where? My ass? I wasn't sure I was ready for that, but I did as I was told. Instead of penetrating my back entrance, however, the guy managed to make a little room for him to slip inside my pussy beside Daemon's cock. I cried out, but this second guy bit down on my shoulder, keeping me still much like an animal does with its mate.

Daemon stroked my hair from my brow, using his big hands to frame my face as he held my gaze. "You can take us, sweet pet. Just take a breath. Let it out." I did as he instructed. Both my feet were on the floor, my legs spread slightly as the men fucked me right there. I had no idea what kind of scene we made but I could imagine. The strobes were still going off and the alcohol was still buzzing me. With that and the sex and the lewdness of the whole situation, I was primed for a carnal explosion.

"Feel good, pet?" Daemon asked as he and the other guy found a rhythm.

"Yes!" My pussy was on fire! And not all of it from the stretching. My clit scraped against Daemon with every movement he made. If he could just move a little faster…

"Blazin is going to come in you first, pet. I'll be staying while others take his place. I will be the last to come. And we will all fill you with our seed. Our scent will be in you. On you. The monsters will know you're ready. Can you handle this?"

I met his gaze boldly. "I can. I will."

He smiled down at me, kissing my nose when I wanted him to take my mouth but it just didn't seem right. I wanted to watch his face as I was fucked and had my pussy and possibly my ass filled with cum while he was still inside me.

The first guy picked up his pace. Daemon nodded over my shoulder and the guy gripped my hips as he pounded inside my pussy. Seconds later he grunted at my shoulder, his cock throbbing inside me. I felt his wet cum bathe me inside, some of it trickling down my leg. He was soon replaced by another man. This one was shorter but still taller than my five foot six frame.

He slid inside me next to Daemon with little trouble, but didn't stay there long. His cock was thick and wet with my juice and the man's cum before him. The head of his dick poked my back entrance, seeking entrance. I pushed out against him, needing him inside me as much as I needed to come.

"That's a good pet," Daemon praised. "Let him have that sweet ass. We'll fill it full too. Before you leave this place, you're going to be full of cum and ready for the night ahead."

I was high. I felt like flying. My head spun as this third guy eased his way into my asshole until I felt his torso against my ass. My dress was bunched at my waist now. Anyone around could see me getting fucked six ways to Sunday. They could see the cum currently dripping down my thigh and the two dicks inside me. It was an invasion, but a welcomed one. One that I craved with every fiber of my being.

That's when I noticed the men around us swapping out dancing partners. Some of them were fucking the women they danced with, just like Daemon was doing to me. Others were simulating it, grinding against their partner with a vigor to match the fast-paced music pounding in the air around us. One girl bent at the waist and took a guy in her mouth while another man slipped inside her, fucking her hard and fast while she swallowed the other guy down greedily.

Then the guy in my ass started his own hard, pounding rhythm. My ass burned, but not unpleasantly so. My pussy throbbed and gripped the cock inside it and I cried out in my shock and pleasure at the new sensations. It was an orgy of the most hedonistic kind. Only when the strobe lights pulsed, the sex around us was normal dancing. I preferred the sex to the dancing.

Seconds later, the guy at my back slammed into me for the final time, roaring his release to the lights above us. A cheer went up as the guy getting blown by the chick being fucked pulled away and took his place behind me.

This time, he went in beside Daemon, both of them sliding in together. I cried out this time. I guess I thought the next man would take my ass again, but apparently, he preferred a hot cunt to a tight ass. I giggled at my own nonsense. I was so overstimulated I wasn't thinking clearly but I loved every fucking second of the dirty, messy sex.

It wasn't long before this guy came in me too.

Then another one. And finally one more. Cum ran down my legs and onto the floor. I was so high strung by this point I was clinging to Daemon. All the while he praised me, but wouldn't give me enough friction to come. Sweat soaked my skin, my hair was plastered to my head, clinging to my face where it touched. My clothes were sticky, not to mention my dress had cum on it. Oh. And I had no panties.

"It's our turn now, pet," Daemon said, his dick still moving inside me.

"I've got cum everywhere," I said, clinging to him as he continued to fuck me.

"I know, sweet. Don't wash when you get home. Keep our cum inside you. I promise you'll have a better night for it if you do. Now. Are you ready to come, pet?"

"Please, yes!" I was past caring who was watching us. I wanted to come and I wanted this guy to come inside me when I did.

Hooking one of my legs over his hip, he angled himself perfectly, then started to fuck me in earnest. Then he *pounded* into me! My cries were loud even over the pulsating music. I gave a thin, keening wail as he fucked me brutally. My pussy was wet with my lust and the cum of several men. Even now, more men surround us. Only Daemon's hiss at them kept others at bay. Apparently, Daemon had decided I'd had enough.

"Now, pet!" he bit out, the command clear. I obeyed.

With a scream, long and loud, I came.

And came and came and came.

Vaguely, I felt Daemon's seed explode inside me, heard his own brutal shout. But all I could process was the orgasm detonating inside me. My legs gave out and another man behind him caught my crumpling form while Daemon finished pumping his cum inside me.

"Easy, pet," the other man said. "I've got you."

I honestly didn't care if he had me or not. I was as weak as a newborn babe. There was no way I could stand on my own.

The second Daemon pulled out of me, the stranger at my back cradled me in his arms and took me to the waiting limo to take me and my friends home. He helped me inside and sent me on my way. Cum was sticky on my thighs and continued to flow from my body with each lingering contraction of my orgasm. It was time to face *him*.

The monster in my closet. Just the thought made me shiver in fear. I'd always hated the dark. Since the dreams started, I hated how horny the thought of him fucking me made me even more than I hated the dark.

I remember walking up my drive after the limo dropped me off, avoiding the shadows, but I didn't really know if I was in any danger from the monster or not. My parents were waiting up, as usual, though Mom didn't seem to notice my clothes were a wreck. I undressed and she helped me to bed, promising to check on me throughout the night. That made me feel better. Not because I was so drunk. Because I was afraid the monster in my closet planned to take me away from my home and everything I'd ever known. If he did, I had no doubt the life he had planned for me wouldn't resemble my old life in the least.

Still buzzing, my pussy still dripping cum, I found myself drifting off into what I hoped would be a night with no dreams.

* * *

"It's time, human." The gruff voice had me gasping in a breath, my eyes flying open. I had no idea how long I was out, but I'd passed out and I was now on my belly. The monster in my closet stood beside my bed, silken cords folded in one hand. Vaguely, the question of what he was going to do with those cords flitted through my mind, but I didn't have to wait long to find out.

Before I could move, he reached for my arms, deadened by my drunken stupor, and tied them behind my back so that my hands grasped my wrists. When I cried out, he placed a gag in my mouth and fastened it securely around my head. Then he did something strange. He straightened my hair so that the gag didn't pull and my hair spilled around my face and back.

I looked up at him, gratitude for that small kindness in my eyes until he grunted. "Need all that pretty hair to hold on to when I'm at your back fucking you."

Tears threatened. I was going to be raped by a monster! I couldn't see him clearly, but his guttural speech and freakishly large size told me he had to be a monster.

"Don't worry, my pretty little pet. You'll be well cared for." *Pretty little pet…* Daemon had called me that repeatedly. He'd also said he was in cahoots with the monster. I'm not sure I really believed anything was real until this moment. I guess I'd find out soon enough. Several of his friends had fucked me. Their cum was still caked on my pussy, ass, and thighs. What if Daemon was wrong, or he had set me up? What if them coming inside me was a really, *really* bad thing?

I started to cry then. This was it. He was really taking me away. I hadn't dreamed this. Unless I was in a nightmare now? I kicked out, adrenaline surging through my veins to give me strength my inebriated body couldn't muster on its own. The monster simply tied my feet at the ankles, then bent my legs and tied my thighs and calves together.

"Ah, very satisfying." His voice, deep and gravelly, brushed my body like a caress. I loved the note that said he truly was satisfied to see me in this shape.

Yep. Had to be in the grip of a nightmare.

With a surprisingly gentle stroke of his hand, the monster petted me from the top of my head, over my back and arms, to settle on my bare ass. I wasn't wearing any panties so there was nothing to impede his exploration. "So soft... so gloriously soft. I bet you're soft all over. Outside... and inside."

I couldn't help the whimper. I just wasn't sure if it was fear.

He chuckled, apparently knowing my dilemma. "Don't worry, my pet. Human females are always undecided. At first. You'll learn to appreciate all we have in store for you."

Wait. *We*? What -- *who* -- the hell was "we?"

Before I had time to truly appreciate all that

implied, the monster picked me up and I landed, still hogtied, over his shoulder. He turned and, wouldn't you just know it, headed for the fucking closet.

Fuck.

He stepped inside and a loud *WHOOSH* assaulted my ears as a violent wind swirled around us. I was trying to scream around my gag when it all abruptly stopped and the monster stepped into a dimly lit, but surprisingly nice, room. It was decorated in rich blues on the walls and floor, but all the furniture and coverings (rugs, drapes, throws) were a deep, scarlet red. Like blood.

"Welcome to your new home, pet," he said, caressing my ass before depositing me gently onto a huge bed. It was truly massive. I'd bet ten monsters his size could easily sleep on it. "You'll have time to explore later. For now, I need to see just what prize I've won."

The monster untied my feet and legs only to retie them. This time, he bent my legs back and tied me so he could spread me wide and place a bar between my ankles to hold me open.

"Nice. Very nice." His voice was less distorted now. Like he'd only partially been in my world and was now fully himself. I craned my neck to look around behind me, needing to get a glimpse of the thing that had me so thoroughly trapped. And abruptly wished I hadn't.

He wasn't human, that was for sure. I remember thinking he had a prominent, almost snout-like nose and mouth structure. It seemed more pronounced now, and he was covered in fur. It was a mixture of blacks, browns, and silvers, as if his pelt couldn't decide what color it wanted to be. His eyes were a fierce golden color, glowing in the dim light. Though he looked like he could kill me as easily as an afterthought, he was surprisingly gentle with his touch. Oh, he didn't seem like the kind of guy who'd let me go if I complained, only that he was the kind of guy who'd check to make sure my skin wasn't mottling under the restraint.

Once he had me positioned where he wanted me -- face down on the edge of the bed -- he squeezed my bare ass. "I'm pleased you came to me without panties." I had the crazy thought to wonder what I looked like to him. Was I wet? Did my lips glisten and beckon him to taste? What about all the dried cum on me? The thought that I was glad I'd shaved my pussy bald flitted through my head before I shut it down.

What? I *did* shut it down! Mostly. OK, so, almost mostly.

"What a juicy little pussy," he growled. "I could just eat it up." He laughed, a deep, rich sound that was both pleasant and sinister. "I smell Daemon's work here." He ran a thick finger from my ass to my cunt, circling the thick tip at my entrance. "In fact, maybe I will. Won't hurt to take a little taste of you before my brothers arrive. I'll make it your reward for submitting to the lesser demons. This is, after all, why they took your virginity."

Brothers? There were more of them? I wanted to question him, but I was still gagged. I guess Daemon told me the truth. Hopefully, he was right in other areas as well. *Fuck.*

Chapter Three

The monster chuckled, the sound oddly erotic. In fact, the longer I was in this position, the more horny I grew. I could feel a breath of pleasantly warm air whisper over my heated skin -- and my weeping pussy -- oddly like a warm summer breeze. Comforting. Soothing. Very pleasant. It eased my fears when it shouldn't have, and when I didn't need soothing. I needed to fight, damn it! Right?

The beast at my back inhaled in a long pull. "Ahhh," he sighed happily. "Smells like an aroused, wet pussy underneath all that cum," he said. "Sweet and juicy."

I craned my neck to look back over my shoulder. He knelt behind me, one knee planted on the bed as he leaned over my ass... smelling my cunt? Yeah. That wasn't embarrassing or anything. I groaned around my gag. "Fuck."

His warm chuckle tickled my pussy because he had his nose mere inches away from my wet flesh. "Later, my pet. But right now, I'm going to taste you. Maybe, if I enjoy your taste, I'll fuck you before my brothers get here. They won't like it, but it's not like they won't have their turn." He waved his hand and, just like in my room when he came, the dripping cum in my pussy and ass evaporated into great puffs of gray and white smoke. Did that clean me? Probably. I'm sure he'd want me clean before he tasted me.

I squeaked. I really needed to find out more about this "brothers" shit. Just exactly what was

expected of me here? What was the monster in my
closet planning on making me do? And did I want to
fight harder? Make my trepidation known?

The monster rubbed my ass, his claws
occasionally digging lightly into my fleshy globes.
"Yeah. Nice and wet. I think my pretty little prize is
going to like it here." Then I felt his furry face
against the cheeks of my ass. Right before his tongue
took a long, slow swipe from my cunt, up the
opening of my pussy, to my ass. "Mmmmm." His
growl was low and long, sending a thrill of
excitement through me. My skin erupted in sweat
and I arched my back as much as I could. Hell, I
even pushed back, trying to get more contact with
my aching cunt.

"Eager little pet. Sexy. You want the monster
in your closet to fuck you?"

Did I? My little whimper said yes even as my
brain tried to scream a resounding, "*Are you fucking
kidding me?*" Somehow, my stupid head nodded
several times instead of shaking the negative
response I should have given. I can only blame the
fact that I was ass up on the bed, most of my weight
on my shoulders with my face pressed into the
mattress. It would have been hard to shake my head.
So I nodded instead. It's the only explanation.

Again, he chuckled, the sound satisfied. "I
knew you'd be like this." He sounded so superior.
Like he'd only been waiting to prove he was right.
"My brothers will be highly pleased."

Again with the brothers thing! I made a noise
behind the gag and he tilted his head at me.

"Wondering what's in store for you? Why I

keep referring to my brothers?"

When I nodded, he grinned even wider. "There are... several of us. We are the rulers of the *Masakh fi Flkhizana* clan." Holy shit! Daemon had been right! "While there are many monsters in closets all over the world, we rule them all. And we just happen to have entry into your dimensional plane from your closet. Each plane has its own gateway, but yours is the strongest." He patted my ass almost affectionately with that big hand of his. "And you are, by far, the most perfect female we've ever come across in the portal to your world. When the leader of all monsters gave us permission to claim a prize for ourselves, we knew what we wanted." He dipped his tongue back to my pussy again for a long, slow, flicking lick. Then he growled. "You."

That low sound vibrating against my pussy just pushed me closer to an edge I wasn't sure I could afford to fall off. He buried his face against my flesh and *slurped*. All the while, he snarled, like I was his very favorite treat in the whole world.

I couldn't help it. I screamed behind the gag, pleasure engulfing me as he licked and ate me out from behind. He left no spot alone either. He swirled his tongue over my asshole and the delicate space below it only to cover my pussy and clit again. It didn't take long before I was dripping with both his saliva and my cunt juice. My clit throbbed and ached even though I was coming harder than I ever had in my life. *And he hadn't even fucked me yet!*

Just as I was coming down from that orgasmic high the monster had taken me to, he gripped my hips and I felt his cock poking me from behind. I chanced a glance over my shoulder and, sure enough, he'd risen behind me, gripped my hips, and was getting ready to shove inside me.

I braced myself just as he took the first plunge. *WHAM!*

With a brutal thrust, he crammed his cock inside me. All the way. I could feel his furry body against my ass! I hadn't seen a lot of cocks to compare it to so I had no real idea what I was dealing with, but it felt simply *massive*. Thank God Daemon and his buddies had taken my virginity and warmed me up for this. My cunt stretched and burned almost unbearably even so, but soon my pussy flooded so that his size was only slightly uncomfortable. At least until he started moving.

Thankfully, once he'd gotten inside me the first time, he was reluctant to leave. At least, that's what it seemed like. He gripped my hips hard and leaned over me, his furry chest tickling my back. One hand slipped around my body, curling around my waist and holding me against him.

"So fucking good," he groaned at my ear. "Our prize is tight and hot."

I cried out, the sound still muffled, and bucked against him, trying to get him deeper. Why I don't know, because he was so big the stretch of his massive cock burned.

"So needy. Can we keep you this way?" He licked my neck, up to the lobe of my ear. "Oh, yes. I think we can. Once I fill you with my cum, you'll be begging for more. Needing to be fucked. Maybe I can sate you. Hmmm? If not... well. We've got all night with you, my pretty little pet."

He lifted himself up and gripped me tight. "Now, little prize." He flexed his hips. "Have you adjusted? Do you need more preparation?"

Preparation? I looked back at him and shuddered. I really needed some more preparation, but how to ask for it?

"Ahh," he said. "You're tender. My cock is bigger than you were prepared for?" He smirked. How could he tell? I certainly couldn't say anything with my mouth gagged. "No worries, little pet." He pulled out and removed the spreader bar from between my ankles. He kept me tied, but flipped me over and shoved my knees up and out. I looked down at my body. My skin was glistening with sweat, my stomach muscles quivering. My arms were still behind me, tied just tight enough to keep me from any movement, but not so harsh it cut off my circulation. I was actually comfortable despite being so restricted.

On my back, I could get a good look at the monster. A *good* look. *All over.*

No wonder it burned when he fucked me. His dick was as big a monster as he was. Long and veiny. Red and angry. It looked as intimidating as the rest of him. And he was about to devour me again.

Dipping his head, the monster did exactly that. My head fell back, and I flexed my hips, trying to get closer to the carnality that was his wicked, wicked mouth and tongue. It felt similar to a human man's tongue -- the one boy who'd clumsily slobbered over me before getting his nut without penetrating me --

but also… different. His snout-like nose tickled as he panted, sniffing me as he lapped. My pussy wept and quivered beneath him, threatening to come with every lash of his tongue. But I didn't. *Couldn't.* Somehow, he kept me on the edge without letting me fall and I knew without a doubt he did it on purpose.

"That's it, pet. That's fucking it," he snarled between my legs. "Feed me cream from your needy little pussy." I did. Because I couldn't help it. He kept lapping at me, bringing my pussy such pleasure, of course it gave him what he wanted!

Licking his lips, he let his gaze dart back up to me, then refocused on my pussy. "Gonna make you come, little pet. One more time. Then I'm gonna fuck you until we both come. You'll adjust to my size." He grinned. "Eventually."

I wanted to ask about the size of the others he'd spoken of earlier, but… hello? Gag!

Again, the monster attacked my cunt. I'd never before felt so out of control. So unable to get a grip on the situation. I was in the arms of a monster! And he was the best lover I'd ever imagined. Any meager experience I'd managed to garner from Daemon and his crew was nothing compared to what I was going through now. I was beginning to suspect I wouldn't miss this for anything in the world.

True to his word, the monster finally brought me over the edge. I screamed behind my gag, arching my back and just letting the explosion happen. My whole body strained with the tension of release. I could actually feel my own cum expelling from my body and onto his waiting tongue. My pussy contracted over and over, grasping for a cock to milk of seed. If the monster was telling me the truth, I'd have one inside me again soon enough.

Finally, he crawled up, bracing himself over me with one hand, and guided his cock into my pussy. When he got more than the head in, he pushed slowly. The look on his face said he was savoring something like heaven. Did he enjoy being inside me that much? He lay on top of me, wrapping both arms around me and holding me to his furry body tightly.

"So good," he growled. "So tight. Hot." He drove into me steadily now, starting a relentless rhythm that threatened to take me into madness again. "So... mine..."

Then he began to fuck me in earnest. The first round had been nothing more than simply getting me used to his cock. To him. Now, he put more effort into it, taking what he wanted. He pounded into me over and over, that big dick plunging in and out of my pussy with ceaseless, pleasurable friction. My clit was on fire. Each time he thrust forward, his fur brushed my clit. Sometimes he angled so there was a firm pressure on me, other times, only the tips of the thick pelt grazed me. It was maddening!

"Unh!!" I cried out behind the gag.

"Fuck!" The monster was panting now, pounding into my helpless body over and over with an animalistic need. "*Fuck*!"

With a brutal yell, my monster plunged into me four more times. On the fifth, he came deep inside my tender pussy. I could do nothing but take what he gave me, tied and helpless as I was. All I could do was come and come and come as he did the same. My pussy welcomed his hot, thick ropes of seed, taking it as greedily as he took me. When he did, the lust that hit me was simply overwhelming. It was like he'd injected me with it, making me incapable of any thought other than the need to come.

Finally, he finished. His body lay over me, his arms clasping me to him as he continued to thrust softly. I felt something inside me swell as the last spurt of his cock filled me. It stretched me, but was so deep I knew there was no way to get him out comfortably. I shifted beneath him, beginning to panic, the lust fading slightly.

"Shh," he said by my ear, lapping and nipping the tender skin at my neck. "We're tied. I'll need to stay inside you for several minutes before we can part."

Tied? *Tied??* Did he just say…

Well… fuck.

Chapter Four

What surprised me the most about this crazy situation was how gentle this monster was. Well, *after* he'd fucked me. No, he didn't untie me or remove my gag. But he rolled us to our sides. My leg was over his thigh and his big hand rubbed from my ass to my knee over and over again. My head lay on his arm and he'd curled it around me. The feeling was languid, making me want to sleep. That hint of lust was still there, but not as strong as it had been when he'd first come. Maybe it was just the eroticism of the moment. He kissed and nuzzled my neck and shoulder, growling low when I moaned in pleasure.

"Dokkin! You motherfucker! We were supposed to do this together! What the fuck?"

"Didn't want to wait, Mikkos. She's smelled too good."

"Yeah, now she fucking smells like your fucking cum. And don't fucking lie. You did it so you'd get a head start on us with the lust madness."

There were several male chuckles. Apparently there was more than just Dokkin, my monster, and Mikkos, another monster.

And just when the fuck did he become *my* monster?

"How much longer you gonna be tied to her?" another one asked. He had a deep, gravelly voice. He sounded calmer than the others but no less intent.

"Another ten minutes, maybe."

"You know, she's got other holes, Fukkon," another one chuckled.

"You're such an ass, Sivyour. Maybe she's not comfortable with that yet?"

"Since when do we fucking care if she's comfortable with it?" I wasn't sure I liked this Sivyour. He *was* an ass. "She's our prize! Who gives a fuck if she's comfortable?"

"Watch your mouth." Dokkin snapped the command, a roar much like that of a wild bear echoed his words like he was half beast. Hell, he was a fucking *monster*! Of course he was a beast! "She's our prize. We earned her with our patience and loyalty. She's to be protected and pleasured."

"She's ours to do with as we please," Sivvour snarled back. Again, the echo of a growl followed his words. "I could give two shits if she's fucking comfortable or not!"

"I'd advise you to take care with your attitude," Fukkon said. His quiet voice was lulling and at the same time arousing. I could listen to this guy read the fucking phone book and get a wettie."

"Fuck you," Sivvour said dismissively as he grasped his cock and gave it several hard tugs. "Daemon said they fucked her good before sending her to us. She can take it." He produced a tiny vial and tipped the contents over the head of his cock. Way more stuff poured out than should have fit in that vial but it was something wet and it was obvious he intended to take my ass so the more the better as far as I was concerned. *And when did I readily accept that I was getting fucked in the ass by a monster?*

Fuck.

Sivvour climbed into bed behind me. Dokkin growled at him, that eerie echoed animal's noise sounding a warning. Sivvour didn't seem to care. He just scooted close to me and guided his cock to the entrance of my ass.

With a shallow thrust, he popped the head of his cock past my ring of muscle. I cried out behind my gag, unsure if the sensation was painful or not. I was certainly full and stretched. It burned mightily, skirting the edge of real pain, but never crossing that line. At least, not yet.

"There," Sivvour said as if he'd proved his point. "She can take me."

"What's your fucking problem, Sivvour? " Dokkin snarled.

"Just proving a point."

"Not with her. She's the only pet we get. If you hurt her and she turns from us, we don't get a second chance."

"We can always cull the bastard," Fukkon said, matter of factly. "I've thought long and hard about this and it may be for the best. Sivvour has always been selfish. He'll never be able to give a pet what she needs."

"Now wait just a Satandamned minute. No one said I was going to run her off. I just want to fuck her ass! Nothing wrong with that! The quicker she gets my cum inside her, the more equal I'll be when she goes lust mad."

"See?" Fukkon raised an eyebrow as if Sivvour had just proven his point. "Always a selfish reason."

"Just do it if you're going to," Dokkin

commanded. "With me inside her like this, I'll be able to better control the situation if it gets out of hand."

"Bastard," Sivvour said but he settled himself in then moved. I still wasn't sure if it hurt or not, but I was trying to reserve judgment. Mainly because the more he moved, the more something was happening inside me. I not only wanted to be fucked in the ass. I needed it.

"You good, pet?" Dokkin kissed my nose as I looked up into his eyes. His face looked less lupine now. The fur on his face receded to a thick beard and long, shaggy hair. His eyes were an icy gold flecked with amber that sparked with intense emotion. Right now, they were bright, but... calm looking?

I nodded, moaning behind the gag. He hesitated, but reached behind my head to remove the blasted thing, then nodded to Sivvour who cut the bonds on my arms. I moved my jaw and licked my lips. Dokkin groaned and took my mouth.

My whole body relaxed into his kiss. Which relaxed my ass around Sivvour's cock.

"Fuck," Sivvour bit out. "She's so fucking tight."

"Responsive, too." Fukkon sat on the edge of the bed watching everything. I saw him just before I closed my eyes and just let them have me.

"There she goes," Dokkin said between kisses. "I'll let her go in a couple more minutes. If I don't fuck her again."

"Don't tie with her again if you do," Fukkon said. "We all need a chance with her before she's overcome with lust. If she imprints, it should be all of us."

Dokkin just growled, but there was no echoing growl. I took that to mean he wasn't really put out. And what did "imprint" mean?

I didn't really have time to worry about it. Because my body was truly surrendering to my monsters. I was limp as a kitten as Dokkin continued to kiss me. I could feel his cock stiffening inside me again while the knot that tied us together lessened its pressure in its shallower position inside my pussy. Dokkin's kiss got more aggressive the longer he continued.

"Fucking tight," Sivvour said through gritted teeth. "She's going to take my cum."

I managed to look back over my shoulder when Dokkin ended his kiss. Sivvour's eyes glowed a reddish amber in his lust. The veins in his neck stood out before his skin disappeared into the fur covering his body. Then he let out a hoarse shout that was echoed by a monstrous, echoed roar.

I cried out as an orgasm crashed into me and I came in a wet rush. I screamed as Dokkin kissed my neck and chin, flexing his hips where he'd grown hard again.

"That's it, my little pet," he purred. "Give us your cum as we give you ours."

The next thing I knew, Fukkon was at my mouth, urging me to take him deep.

There was a derisive snort somewhere in the room. "Always looking out for everyone else, eh, Fukkon? Looks to me like you want to use her just as much as the rest of us." The tone was snippy and grouchy.

"Just come get your part, Mikkos. There's enough for everyone." Dokkin continued to pet me while he fucked me in a lazy glide. With Fukkon above us at the head of the bed, his cock crammed down my throat, I was surprised at how well I was taking it all. But then, something was happening to me. I couldn't seem to get enough of the monsters. The longer it continued, the more I craved them. Most of all, I craved their cum. It was all I could think about.

"Oh, God!"

"Pet, God has nothing to do with this. This is all Lucifer. He made us." He urged me to look at him even as Fukkon continued to fuck my mouth. "So beautiful," he purred. "Eager for our cum, hmm?"

All I could do was whimper. Fukkon had started out gentle in fucking my mouth, but now he was grunting and his thrusts were becoming more and more aggressive. He hit the back of my throat with each surge forward, making me gag sometimes. He didn't let up, though, nor did I want him to. I simply turned my head up to him so he could thrust deeper.

"That's it, pet. Suck him down." Dokkin stroked the hair from my face and scooped the saliva from my chin to feed it back to me around Fukkon's cock. "Suck him good and he'll feed you his cum. Would you like that?" His words were crude but gentle. As if he were offering me my favorite treat if I'd just do what he asked. Just thinking about it made my mouth water. I did want Fukkon's cum. In fact, I wanted them all.

I moaned and opened my mouth wider, sticking out my tongue. I felt another monster at my back, cramming his cock into my ass. The cum from Sivvour eased the way for this guy. I could only assume it was Mikkos, but I wasn't sure. When he surged inside me, he did so with all the finesse of an elephant in a china shop. There was no easing his way inside, letting me adjust. He simply took what he wanted with a grunt and an echoing growl.

Dokkin chuckled, then started to move inside me once again. The sawing motion between him and Mikkos was uneven and independent of each other. Mikkos's breath was heavy in my ear. His tongue darted out to lap at the skin of my shoulder several times.

"So fucking sweet," he said, nipping my neck and leaving a little stinging bite there. His mark? "I'll fuck that sweet pussy when that bastard, Dokkin, isn't hogging it all. When I do, I'll make you fucking scream."

His words set me off, just as Fukkon let his head fall back on a brutal yell. Instantly, I was filled with his cum, trying to swallow every drop. I gulped and swallowed as he emptied himself. I took him deep to the back of my throat. I felt the head of his cock pressing against me when I swallowed, triggering my gag reflex. But I didn't lose a drop. I opened my mouth wider for a moment, gasping in great gulps of air, still swallowing like mad. When all he was giving me were drops of his salty cream, I sucked harder. My lips were stretched, but I latched on to the head and sucked for all I was worth.

"AHH!" Fukkon's cry was punctuated by an

echoed roar that only encouraged me to keep going. "Fucking girl's got a mouth on her!" He didn't sound like the reasonable, level headed monster he'd been at first. He sounded on the verge of being out of control. "Satandamn mother fuck! FUCK!" He roared and I got a fresh infusion of cum from him. Not as much as the first time, but enough I got a good drink, swallowing as hard and fast as I could. He had to forcefully pull out of my mouth this time, a little *pop* sounding when he broke the suction of my lips.

Fukkon collapsed back onto the bed above us but I was too busy to see exactly what he did. I grabbed Dokkin's beard and pulled him to me for a kiss. I still had Fukkon's cum in my mouth and the monster shared it with me.

At first he seemed surprised, but must have decided to roll with it as I kept kissing him, licking at his tongue and nipping his lip when he tried to pull back.

"Looks like the little bitch already has you tamed, Fukkon," Sivvour said as he stroked himself, apparently readying for another round. "Sucked you dry twice."

Fukkon gasped for breath, his hand still in my hair, grasping reflexively. "Don't care if she does." There was a contented purring echo to his words this time. "That mouth is a fucking miracle."

"I'll be the judge of that," Sivvour said as he took Fukkon's place at my mouth. I greedily reached for him, pulling his hardening cock into my mouth and took him as far as I could. I swallowed, milking the head of his cock with my throat. "Mother fuck!"

Fukkon barked out a laugh. An echo followed and somewhere in my lust filled mind, and I realized the echo accompanied sharp emotion. At least I'd always know when they were serious. "Told you."

"Fucking heaven!" Sivvour found my hair and gripped tight, pulling at my scalp. "That's fucking good! Suck my dick, you slut!"

OK, so, I'm not a slut. I've never been called a slut and never wanted to be a slut. There was a surge of anger inside me... that quickly turned into a violent lust I had no hope of controlling.

Before I could stop myself, I pulled Sivvour's cock from my mouth and gave it a healthy smack before sucking it back in. Sivvour's reaction was to gasp in surprise, echoed by a small whimper, echoed by an animalistic growl.

"Oh, I see I hit a nerve." His voice was menacing, his teeth bared. His grip on my hair tightened and he forced more of his dick down my throat. "Fuckin *whore*," he said with some force, emphasizing the "whore" part. "You suck my dick until I fucking shoot my cum down your fucking throat!"

Sivvour repositioned his hands on either side of my face and fucked my mouth, holding me still to take whatever he wanted to give me. Tears leaked from my eyes down my cheeks from the choking, and saliva dripped steadily from my chin.

With Dokkin in my pussy and Mikkos in my ass, there was no way I could truly do anything. They were taking from my tender body anything their monstrous selves wanted.

"Fuck, that's hot," Fukkon said as he moved off the bed to slide below us. "Her pussy and ass being fucked. Her mouth being used just as hard. And she's fucking taking it!"

"You expected less?" Dokkin bit out the words, his voice sounding strained. "She's our choice. Meant for us."

"Yeah, well, you better hurry and fill her. She's gonna need all the lust she has in that tight little body in a minute. *He's* coming."

As one, the three monsters fucking me groaned.

"Fuck that shit," Sivvour said, fucking my mouth all the harder. "I'm coming whether he's here or not. He can fucking wait his turn." But he sped up, his cock throbbing like mad in my mouth. He was swelling, getting ready to come. So I fluttered the underside of his cock with my tongue before swallowing him deep.

With a sharp cry, Sivvour ejaculate. Hard. His cum slid down my throat without me having to swallow. I just opened my mouth as best I could and let it slide down. Some escaped and dribbled down my chin, but Fukkon was there to feed it back to me.

Dokkin and Mikkos both gripped my hips, holding me still, and pounded into my body mercilessly. Each had his own rhythm so they seemed to have a tug-of-war going with me. But soon, both monsters shot their loads into my body, filling me with monster cum once again.

"Fuck…" Dokkin groaned. "Motherfuck!"

"Same," Mikkos said, panting. "Gonna enjoy this fuck toy. Hot little piece."

Then the door opened.

"Y'all coulda waited on me, you dumbshits."

The accent was distinctly... hillbilly? What the fuck?

Chapter Five

I looked toward the new voice and nearly lost my mind. The guy was head and shoulders bigger than any of the monsters in the room and twice as wide. In short, he was fucking *huge*! Muscles roped every limb and his torso. He had on briefs, but they did nothing to cover the massive erection he sported. And it was growing harder by the second.

"Well, shit," Dokkin muttered. "I thought you were exploring the Under realm."

"Yeah, well, ain't none of 'em worth killin'. Besides, I got the feelin' y'all were tryin' to pull somethin' on me. Now I see you were tryin' to get a pet to imprint you before I had my share."

"Hey, you left us, motherfucker," Sivvour said, pointing a finger at the big guy. A small roar echoed his words.

"You're an asshole bastard moron!" the big guy snarled. An even bigger roar echoed his words. "And you're a jealous motherfucker at that. You can't stand it that I'm bigger'n stronger'n you so you're all the time tryin' ta make me look dumb. I left 'cause I got tired'a your fuckin' shit!" Roars and snarls echoed all around. Apparently this was a hot topic for all of them.

"Now let's all just calm down," Dokkin said, trying to keep his voice calm but there was a soft snarly echo. "Are you staying this time, Bob? Because if not, you don't get to --"

"Wait," I said, sitting up on the bed, batting Dokkin's hand away when he would have just shoved me back down. "Your name is Bob?"

There was silence. No one said a for long moments. Then, "Ain't nothin' wrong with 'Bob.'"

"No," I said. "There's not. It's just a name I can actually pronounce. How'd you get that name when all the others are so, I don't know, *monsterish*?"

That seemed to be the exact right thing to say to take the tension out of Bob. He grinned, taking a couple steps toward the bed. "See, that's what I told them when pickin' out our names eons ago. You want something people can pronounce. So, Satan, in reward for me bein' so much fuckin' smarter than these assholes, made me the biggest and the strongest."

"And the stupidest," Sivvour muttered.

Bob lunged for Sivvour and backhanded him across the room. A deafening roar echoed throughout the chamber and I clapped my hands over my ears with a cry. Dokkin leapt from the bed to put himself between me and Bob, followed closely by Mikkos, while Fukkon covered me bodily.

"You fuckers," Bob growled. "You know I ain't gonna hurt her."

"No," Dokkin said. "But I'd prefer she not get splattered in Sivvour's blood and guts."

Sivvour bared his teeth at everyone. "I found the bitch. And this is the thanks I get?"

"You're an asshole," Mikkos said. "Always have been."

"Well, every single one of you guys can suck my dick."

"Dear God," I muttered. "I'm a babysitter."

That got everyone to shut up.

"I beg your pardon?" Dokkin turned to face me. "A babysitter?"

I shoved Fukkon off me and got to my knees. One hand went to my pussy where I still dripped cum. "Well, what the fuck would you call it? I'm sitting here, hornier than I've ever been in my life, pumped full of cum, with one only fucking guy in this room I've yet to fuck. And you guys are fussing about who left who or who found who, or anything other than actually fucking me." I pounded my chest with one fist. "I'm the fucking pet here. You will pay attention to me or I will destroy things."

Bob threw back his head and laughed until tears ran down his cheeks and he had to wipe them with the back of his arm. His dick was even harder -- and bigger -- than before.

"Who the fuck can argue with that?" He lost his shorts and crawled up on the bed. "Come here, little pet. It's my turn to pump you full."

"Good," I said, reaching for him. As he covered me, I grasped his cock with one of my hands. It was hard, veiny, and so thick I had no hope of wrapping my fingers around it. "Because I'm getting even more horny by the second. And I want this big, fat cock stuffing me full."

Bob grunted, wedging the head of his cock at my pussy opening. "I'm a big fucker," he said softly. "If you can't take me, I understand." The big guy actually sounded dejected.

"For fuck's sake." I shoved, and Bob rolled off me. No doubt he did it because he thought he was hurting me because no way could I move him off me if he didn't want to be moved.

Without missing beat, I straddled him. When I sat down, nestling his dick between my pussy lips, that big cock jerked so hard, it actually lifted me.

"Now," I said. "Shut up."

I rose up on my knees and grasped his cock, pointing it straight up. Then I impaled myself on it, sliding ever downward until I was stuffed with monster cock, my thighs flush against his fuzzy hips. The more turned on Bob got, the more his fur appeared.

Not wasting any time, I started moving, bouncing up and down on his veiny shaft. He panted and grunted with every rise and fall of my body on his. The invasion in my pussy stretched me a ridiculous amount, and it burned, but the fuck if I cared! It felt fucking good!

Bob grasped my thighs and pulled me down with each passing second until finally, he moved his grip to my hips and started just lifting me. Each time he pulled me back, he surged up into me. It made for a teeth clattering ride.

"FUCK!" Bob roared as he shoved me off him, rolling me to my belly and pulling my ass high in the air. He mounted me from behind, gripped my hips, and fucked the ever-loving shit out of me. Our bodies slammed together in a violent conflagration, the teeth clattering ride he gave me more than I'd ever expected. I could feel him hitting me high inside with nearly painful intensity. I was half afraid he'd hurt something up there, half afraid he'd stop this mad fucking. Because, God (or Satan) help me, I fucking *loved it*!

It wasn't long before his snarls and growls

grew animalistic and so loud I was afraid to look over my shoulder for fear of what I'd see. I was sure he was in the grip of his monster transformation, and I wasn't sure I was ready to see that. But I didn't have to worry. I was too busy coming and coming and coming around that big monster cock. Every pulse of his cock stretched and stimulated my clit. Every time that happened, it set off an explosion inside me.

Finally, Bob gripped my hips and was thrusting so hard he propelled me across the bed. I nearly fell, but he scrambled off and just wrapped his arms around me, lifting me off the ground. I was still impaled on that gigantic cock of his, my feet not touching the floor.

Bob continued to surge inside me, fucking me for all he was worth. He was like a jackhammer inside me he moved so fast. I screamed, thrashing my head and trying to grip his body with my legs but unable to cross my ankles together. I settled for hooking his thighs with my feet so the angle let him continue to fuck me as ruthlessly as he wanted. I felt like I was being torn in two, but like I was getting ready to come a flood all at the same time.

Bob's breaths came faster and faster until he threw back his head and roared so loud dust fell from the ceiling. My scream lasted longer than his, but we both came so hard I have no idea how either of us was conscious. Bob's cum flooded my cunt to overflowing. Cum trickled from my pussy, down his balls, to the floor in a steady stream. My own cum mingled with his, and yes, I truly did come a flood.

The next thing I knew, Dokkin lifted me gently

and cradled me in his arms. Fukkon waved his hand, and I was at once clean and comfortable, no evidence of monster cum in or on my body that I could tell. I was completely exhausted.

"You did so good, little pet," Dokkin praised. "So very good. You'll be ours forever."

"Will you fuck me some more?" I asked weakly.

Dokkin chuckled. "Every night, multiple times a night, until you're the one seeking us for sex. Then we'll fuck you even more."

"Is that what imprinting is?"

"Yes, little pet. When you can't imagine your life without at least one of us fucking you every second of every day. The more you imprint, the more monsters there will be to satisfy you. But you also have to be able to take our cocks. Some humans can't."

I looked up at him in confusion. "But I did. I took you all."

"That you did, pet. You've almost there. Now, we wait. You'll go back to your realm during the day, but at night, you're ours. If you get to a point where you can't make it without sex until we come for you at night, you find Daemon. If that still isn't enough, he'll get the other lesser demons. If you still aren't satisfied, you'll have finished the imprinting and you'll be ours forever."

"Every second of every day," I said drowsily. "Sex." I sighed happily. "Fucking. I want to fuck all the time if it makes me feel like this."

Mikkos chuckled. "Little wanton. I think she'll be fine."

"I think so, too," Dokkin said. Then he kissed me. "Time to go back, pet. I'll come for you tomorrow night. Then we'll see how much you want to fuck."

I turned to Bob who was sitting on the bed, his breath still heaving. "Will you fuck my ass tomorrow? I really need you to cum in me there."

He barked out a laugh. "Yeah, pet. I'll fuck your ass. In fact, I think tomorrow I'll come in all your holes. And on your body."

"That sounds nice," I said, yawning. "Cum all over me... In me..." I was drifting off.

"It does indeed," Dokkin said. "Until tomorrow, sweet pet."

Then I slept the most peaceful, restful sleep I'd ever had.

I could only wonder what tomorrow would be like. Hopefully, I'd find Daemon or his crew and see if they could still fuck me. Yeah. That was a good idea. Best. Birthday. *Ever*!

Seduced From The Monster In My Closet
(Monster World 2)
By Wanda Violet O.

I have no idea if the monsters are real, but I know my body feels the delicious pain this morning. Not nearly satisfied, I look for other means of release. Which is how I ended up a play thing for the same man who took my virginity in a dance club the night before. Only this time, the servants are out to seduce me away from my monsters. Will I go willingly? Do I even have a choice?

WARNING: This is a short erotica novella... if you want a strong plot and character development, you won't find them here. What you will find is hot sex and one satisfied woman -- with a monster out of the closet and in her bed... along with a few other beings.

Chapter One

I woke with a gasp, my eyes wide, my gaze darting around my room. The sun was just peeking over the gently rolling hills visible in my bedroom window. A smoky haze rose from my naked body as I lay in a tangled mess with the covers on my bed.

The monsters!

Immediately, I jumped up from the bed and made a beeline to the closet. Throwing it open, I shoved clothes out of the way, trying to see if my dream was real or the made-up imaginings of my drunken state the night before. There's nothing in the small space that looked even remotely suspicious. I sank to the floor and groaned softly.

What the fuck happened last night? My body was deliciously sore, so I knew I'd been fucked. But by who? With the reality of daylight slowly dawning, I wasn't sure I wanted the answer to that question. I vaguely remember my mother helping me to bed, but I wasn't sure how much she was aware of. A quick glance at the clock said it was six in the morning. Good. I needed to assess the damage and decide if I'm crazy or just horny as fuck.

Getting my feet, I went to my bathroom. Thankfully I had one adjoining my bedroom. I examined myself, sitting in front of the full-length mirror on the back of the door. I spread my legs and part my pussy lips. I'm pink and swollen. Definitely well used. Turning around, I spread my ass cheeks, my shoulder on the floor so I can look behind myself at the reflection of my gaping ass. Definitely been fucked there too. Though there were twinges of pain, there's no blood and doesn't appear to be any damage. As I inspected myself, however, my pussy started to cream and my asshole winked at me in the mirror.

Yeah. I'm a total slut. Can you see my goofy smile?

Unable to resist, I reached behind me and inserted two fingers in my asshole. They slid right in with little resistance. So I added a third. I felt full, my ass stretching and burning slightly, but I loved that little burn.

I remember the night before when I'd been desperate to rid myself of my virginity, I'd longed for a toy so I could just do it myself. Now, I wished for a toy so I could just get myself the fuck off. I was horny in a way I could never remember being and it was getting worse by the second.

With nothing to fuck myself with other than my fingers, I reached between my legs -- my ass still in the air and the fingers of my other hand still deeply seated there -- I thrust three fingers deep inside my cunt. I could tell there was no way for me to actually get off like this, but I loved watching myself in the mirror and I had to do fucking something. I was horny as a motherfucker with no relief in sight.

Yeah. I really needed to find that guy from last night at the club. I had no idea if the monster in my closet was real, or if there were really five of them instead of just the one. I'd come to look forward to seeing the past few months, but I knew there was a human man out there somewhere who'd fucked me last night and I wanted a repeat.

I continued to fuck myself, experimenting with my fingers in my ass and pussy. I wanted to be fucked hard. To have my body used like it had been last night on my twenty-first birthday. There had been multiple men fucking me. In both holes. Right there on the dance floor. I wondered if my dress still had cum stains on it. I hoped it was in my bedroom because explaining those stains to my mother wasn't something I wanted to do.

Rubbing and stroking my pussy made me wet. My fingers gleamed with my juice as I dragged them through it. I did this over and over, occasionally circling my clit until I managed to get four fingers in my little pussy.

This was extreme. Even for a girl who'd let a stranger take her virginity. In the middle of a dance floor. I removed the fingers from my ass and just concentrated on fucking my cunt. Turning over to my side, I reached behind me to find my cunt again. I stretched and twisted my hand until all four fingers could move in and out of my pussy easily to my thumb. God, that looked hot! Felt naughty and darkly pleasurable, too. As I continued to fuck my hand half way inside me, the sight mesmerized me.

My phone rang, breaking my concentration. I hadn't even remembered putting it in the bathroom, but it was there on the vanity. The ring tone was *This is Halloween* as covered by Marilyn Manson. What the actual fuck? I'd never had that ring tone before.

A wave a guilt and shame washed over me. What was I doing? My pussy ached and throbbed, but not all of it was pleasure. There was a very real discomfort born from my desperate attempt to get myself off. All of a sudden, my attempt at self fisting wasn't as erotic as it was stupid. This time yesterday I was a virgin, for crying out loud! Now I was into extreme self pleasure? Yeah. Needed to lay off the booze.

I hastily washed my hands before I picked up my phone. The name on the caller ID stuck out at me. *Daemon…*

I swallowed. Was this… *my* Daemon? The man who'd fucked me last night on in the club? "H-hello?"

A warm, vaguely sinister chuckle greeted me. "My pretty little pet."

"Oh, my God," I gasped. "You're… you're real?"

"Why pet, I think I'm hurt. You didn't believe I was real?" His voice was smooth as honey. Seductive in the extreme. If I remembered him correctly, there was a time during the night when he'd said he worked for the monsters in my closet, but I was far from sure. Hell, if he'd said that, he could well have been playing with me. Making fun of me.

"I was a bit drunk," I mumbled out. "But never mind that. Where are you?" I needed to find this guy. Stat!

Again, he chuckled. "My, we're demanding this morning. What is it you require, little pet?"

"I want… I want you to fuck me again." I took a breath. "Can we meet?"

"Of course. I'm here to serve. When would my pet want to meet me?"

"The sooner the better. I'm... well, I'm horny. Like really horny. I need to fuck." Had I not been so desperate, I'm sure I'd never have been so forward. Or vulgar. Maybe. I was beginning to think I wasn't the good girl I'd always pretended to be.

"Well then. I won't keep my pet waiting." My phone gave a little chime. "I've sent you directions to my home. Come to me when you're ready. I'll do all your heart desires."

"Anything?"

"Anything and everything, my pet."

I ended the call and hurried to dress. Yoga pants and a sweater for the cool air. I didn't need anything else because I didn't plan on wearing anything that long.

Scribbling a hastily written note to my parents about going to a friend's house, I snagged my keys and bolted out the door. I had a full tank of gas, so I didn't have to worry about that. Thank goodness too because, looking at the map on my phone, the place Daemon was sending me to was a good hour out of the city.

When I pulled up to the gated property, I was in awe of the wealth demonstrated. A guard stuck his head out of the gatehouse and I rolled down my window.

"Private property, Miss," he said. "Go back down the primary drive."

"Daemon gave me directions to come this way."

The guard raised an eyebrow. "Daemon? You're Wyn?"

I stuck my chin up. "I am."

He smirked at me as he opened the electronic gate. "Welcome, pet. Enjoy your time here."

I had the feeling there was more going on than I knew but I honestly didn't care. I was here to get fucked. I honestly didn't care who did the fucking as long as it was long, hard, and good.

I drove down the long winding drive to the main house. There were several cars parked out front, but I was directed to a long stretch of red carpet that led up the steps to the house. A tall, good looking attendant stood ready to open my car door as I pulled up.

He reached for my hand and helped me to my feet, saying, "Welcome. My name is Sammael. Daemon has requested you leave your clothes in your car. He says you won't need them." He smiled kindly. "If the carpet is not thick enough and your feet encounter something hurtful, like a pebble, I'm to carry you. He has no wish for you to be harmed, including being uncomfortable with your nudity. He will allow no one to humiliate you in any way. This is about fun."

That wasn't expected, but I was past caring. The long drive to the house and my unfulfilled lust from earlier had left me nearly panting with need. Besides, I'd already acknowledged I hadn't planned on wearing my clothes long. As to the humiliation part, I was glad of it. That might have been the one thing that could have turned off this lustful need I had inside me, but, if it didn't, I wasn't sure I could handle it afterwards.

Chapter Two

Without hesitation, I shrugged off my sweater and bra, then lost my pants, panties, and slip-on shoes. Sammael took my hand and placed it in the crook of his arm, beaming down at me with a satisfied smile. "It's a good day for pleasure," he murmured. "I guarantee you, you will pleased this day, pet."

I looked up at him, startled by his use of the word pet to address me. The guard at the gate had as well. Inside me, my stomach did a slow roll. Just what exactly was in store for me today? It made my pussy weep in anticipation wondering about it.

Once inside, Sammael took me to a large room past the foyer of the house. The predominant color was a deep, deep scarlet. The floors were covered in plush carpet, and the walls had a heavy covering the same color with intricate textures over them. The couches and chairs and any rugs were a deep ebony and any fixtures or edging were done in a rich, shiny gold. Only the ceiling was a gentle cream color.

Around the room were different unique pieces of furniture that I suspected weren't normal furniture. All of them had fur lined padded benches and gold rings at various places that looked like they might be there to restrain someone. There was a large wardrobe in one corner that was a very imposing piece. I could easily imagine it being filled with toys and whips and chains and crops... All in all, it looked like what it was probably going to be. A den of iniquity.

Sammael continued to hold my hand resting in the crook of his arm as if he didn't want to let it go. The smile on his face was smug and almost prideful as he walked us to the center of the room.

"May I present, Miss Wyn."

"Ah, my beautiful pet." Daemon rose from a chair in the corner as if he'd just been waiting for Sammael to introduce me. "So lovely to see you again." His gaze raked over my naked body. Unable to resist, I put my shoulders back a little, knowing the movement would lift my breasts just that little bit. I lifted my chin in confidence, very much unlike the pet he called me.

"I'm glad to see you, too," I said softly. I took a breath, closing my eyes. I was so wound up I could feel the moisture dripping from my cunt down my inner thigh.

When I opened my eyes again, Daemon was standing in front of me, a soft smile on his face. "Don't be afraid, my pet. Though I will push your boundaries, I would never hurt you or allow you to be hurt.

"I know. I wouldn't have come otherwise." OK, that was a lie. I knew it the moment I opened my mouth to utter it but didn't stop myself from saying it.

Immediately, Daemon's visage hardened. "You will not lie to me, Wyn," he bit out. "Not ever. It is essential to keep you safe."

I winced. "Sorry," I said. "I honestly didn't realize it was a lie until just before I said it." I looked up at him, not hiding my need. "What's happening to me?"

His expression softened. "Ah, the imprinting is going quicker than they thought." He shook his head slightly. "Quicker than any other prize I've ever heard of." Then his expression turned cunning. "I can use that. You can too, pet. That's assuming you still want to do this."

"I don't know what I'm doing, so how can I know what I want?" Suddenly, I felt almost desperate. With lust, yes. But something else, too. "What's happening to me, Daemon?" I took the step separating us and coiled my arms around his neck, rubbing my naked body against his fully clothed one. The texture of the fine material was rough enough to make my nipples ache as it scraped over them. I moaned as I leaned up to kiss him.

At first, he dodged my lips. "No, pet," he whispered. "That's not mine to take."

"Why?" I whimpered, feeling like I needed that kiss or I'd die.

"Your sweet kisses…" He closed his eyes and winced slightly. "Dokkin will not be happy," he muttered.

My eyes widened. "He's real?"

"Oh, yes, my pet. He and his brothers are very real."

I stuck my chin out. "Then why did they send me back?" I shivered in Daemon's arms. I've never felt so out of control in my life! "If I'm supposed to be theirs, if they knew this was going to happen to me, they should have kept me with them if they didn't want me to find a way to get some relief! I can't make it until tonight!"

Daemon put me at arm's length, looking down

at me with a very serious expression. "Are you telling me the monster clan is not taking care of you properly? Not meeting your needs?" I opened my mouth to brush it off. I wouldn't say it was as serious as that, but it hurt that they'd leave me here so in need with no way to get relief. He shook his head and continued. "You must speak the truth, Wyn, always. If you need to explain your answer, fine. But you must speak the truth."

"Well, then no. I don't suppose they are taking care of me properly. Dokkin said he'd come for me tonight, but I can't wait until tonight."

"Because you're looking forward to their attentions?"

I shook my head almost violently. "No! Because I'm so horny I can't see straight! It gets worse with every second! When you called me, I'd been up exactly fifteen minutes. And I'd locked myself in the bathroom and was on the floor in front of my mirror watching as I did my best to cram my whole hand up my cunt! I even had three fingers in my ass at one point! *And I still haven't gotten off!*" Tears spilled from my eyes down my cheeks and I shivered violently.

"Fucking bastards," Daemon swore.

Sammael was now at my side, his big hands rubbing from my neck to my shoulders and down my arms before sliding back up. Over and over he did this, occasionally dipping his lips to my neck for a gentle kiss. I soaked up the attention, but the tactile sensations made my lust even worse.

"I see no reason to change our plans for her," Sammael said softly. "Their loss is our gain."

"We still need a reason. We'll have to plead our case if she imprints wholly." Daemon sounded like he was planning through their course of action. I looked up at him waiting. His hands gripped my hips before sliding around to my ass almost absently. Then he seemed to come to a decision. "Fuck them," he said. "She needs. We provide. It's been our way for thousands of years."

"Good," Sammael said as he turned me around, lifting me in his arms so my body was flush against his. My legs went around his hips automatically, followed by me grinding my clit as hard as I could on the ridge of his cock. As he took me to a large couch, his mouth covered one of my tits, sucking as much of one small breast into his mouth as he could. I cried out and wrapped my arms around his head, holding him to me. When he let go of my tit with a little pop, he grinned up at me. "Delicious."

"Prepare her, Sammael," Daemon said. "Today, she gets everything she wants. I want her to come so hard she passes out."

"My pleasure," Sammael said as he licked his lips.

He laid me on a long futon, spreading my legs so that one draped over the back and the other suspended over the edge. Before I could appreciate exactly what was going to happen, Sammael practically dove between my legs, putting his mouth over my cunt to suck strongly.

"Fuck!" I gasped as I threaded my fingers through his hair, thrusting my pussy at his face while he licked and sucked. "So fucking good!"

"Take her over a couple of times, Sammael," Daemon said as if he were talking about something that happened every day. "Let her come quickly. We'll make her last longer later."

That sounded just about perfect to me.

Sammael just grunted before setting in to feast on my cunt in earnest. He licked and sucked, milking both cream and screams from me with effortless ease. The first orgasm hit me in a matter of seconds. The next one wasn't far behind. I was so wound up, a cool breeze would have set me off.

I lay there just *feeling*. Letting Sammael take over. At one point, I pulled my knees up so they were beside my shoulders and Sammael had easy access to my wide-open pussy. The growls and grunts coming from between my legs were a major turn on. He obviously enjoyed what he was doing because the longer he kept at it, and the more juice I fed him from my little pussy, the wilder he sounded, and the rougher he tongued and sucked me. He even nipped me sharply several times only to suck and tongue me to soothe the ache. Then he stabbed three fingers into my open cunt. I screamed, pulling my knees wider apart and thrusting my hips at those plundering digits.

"Like that, do you." His voice was rough and animalistic. The Sammael who was so gentle and kind when he helped me into the house was gone. In his place was a man determined to drive me out of my mind.

"More!" I screamed. "Give me more!"

He smacked my ass. Hard. "You're not in control here," he snapped. "You'll take what I give you, when I give it to you."

The sharp pain contrasted with the wonderful pleasure of his mouth on my cunt pushed me over again. "Oh, God! Fuck! Yes!"

"Spank her again," Daemon said. I glanced up, nearly desperate to find his gaze and there he was. Standing over me. Still fully clothed, but he'd taken his cock out of his fly and was stroking the thick, veiny length. There was a drop of precome hanging on the head and I longed to taste it. I hadn't realized I'd stuck out my tongue, begging for him, until Daemon grinned. "Eager to take my cock down your throat, little pet?" I nodded eagerly. "Sammael, turn her around. I want her head hanging off the edge so I can feed her my cock."

Sammael did as instructed, moving me so that my legs were over the back of the couch and my head was down. Daemon gripped the back of my neck with both hands, holding me steady as he lay his dick on my cheek, rubbing the precome on my face. "Open for me, beautiful pet. This can be as gentle or as rough as you want. But" -- he grinned down at me -- "I have a feeling you need it just a little bit rough."

"Yes, Daemon," I gasped out, turning my head, trying to get his cock in my mouth. "I need it hard and rough. Make me gag on it."

His chuckle sounded almost sinister. Which only made me cream for him more. "One step at a time, pet. Soon, you'll be gagging more cocks than just mine. We have a long day ahead of us.

He wasn't lying.

Feeding his cock into my mouth, Daemon held

me still with his hand at the back of my neck. Slowly, he thrust, sliding more of his cock into my mouth with each thrust.

At first, I tried to wrap my lips around him, but A: he was too big, and B: I didn't want to hurt him with my teeth. Finally, I settled for just opening my mouth and letting him do as he wished. Then things went faster. Before I knew it, he was sliding his dick down my throat with ease all the way to the base. I did, indeed, gag. Several times. Then I learned how to relax my throat and all I had to worry about was the excess saliva. Things were definitely going to be messy.

He went slow, giving me time to prepare for each thrust. But as I relaxed into the movement, he started going faster. And faster. I had trouble with the saliva but he'd just stop and say, "Spit," and I'd spit it out. Sometimes, it fell to the floor. Sometimes it landed on his dick. That was the hottest of all. Then he'd feed the sloppy mess back to me when he put his cock back in my mouth.

My legs spread wide with Sammael eating my pussy like no tomorrow, Daemon fucking my face until I gagged -- even pushing me through it until I relaxed again -- had me so fucking horny I wanted to scream. If I, you know, hadn't had a fat dick stuck down my throat. I did scream around his dick, but it came out as "gac, gac, gac" as he fucked me.

"Hot as fuck," a voice beside us said. I couldn't see, but it wasn't a man's voice. It was pitched high and sounded young, but with a sensual note that only stirred my lusts even more. "You gonna let me play, too? She's so wound up, she needs a woman's touch to keep from breaking."

"You're welcome to join us, Lillith," Daemon said through gritted teeth. "As soon as I come in her mouth, you can kiss her until the two of you eat it all up."

I squealed, another orgasm shooting through me as Sammael kept licking and slurping at my pussy. His fingers played inside me perfectly, but I still wanted more. I needed fucked.

In my pussy.

In my ass.

My face.

I wanted it all.

Chapter Three

When I squeezed around Daemon's cock, he buried himself deep. My nose rested on the underside of his heavy balls. I couldn't breathe, but I didn't care. I knew he wouldn't give me anything I couldn't take. And if he did, I wasn't certain I cared right now. I was needy. Horny beyond caring about anything other than what depraved act of sex would get me off.

With a long, loud grunt, Daemon came, his cum exploding inside my mouth. I swallowed some of it, but some leaked out at the corners around his dick. He still held himself in for long moments. I lay passively taking all he had to give me.

When he backed out slowly, a woman moved in to replace his dick with her mouth, kissing me deeply. We swapped his cum between us and she moaned as much as I did.

"Mmmm, you taste good, pussycat." She had deep ebony skin, long braids, and the most startling copper eyes I'd ever seen, shining like new pennies. Even though I'd only caught a fleeting glimpse of her before she began kissing me so passionately, I knew she was flawless. I was acutely aware of the mess my face was after the harsh round of oral sex. "So beautiful," she murmured between kisses. She kept lapping delicately but insistently at the inside of my mouth, licking saliva and cum from my lips and face. "You're perfect for us, pussycat. I'm looking forward to lapping up the cream our men coax from you. Or the cream I coax myself," she purred.

I could do nothing but open my mouth and let her do as she wished. Sammael was still finger fucking me and sucking my clit wickedly while the woman continued to kiss me. When Sammael pressed a fourth finger into my aching cunt, I came again. Explosively.

Lillith petted my face as I screamed and screamed. My throat was raw with my screams before the orgasm began to fade. My ears rang and roared, my vision tunneling.

The next thing I knew, I was lying flat on the couch again, my head in Daemon's lap. Lilith was settling herself between my legs, idly stroking my clit with her fingers and occasionally licking it with her little tongue. I looked up at her, a sense of wonder overtaking me. She placed little kisses over my inner thighs as she continued to help me ride out the last of my orgasm. "You're beautiful," I said because I couldn't help myself.

She smiled up at me. "As are you." She lapped at my pussy and I shivered. "You like it when a woman eats you out?"

"I've never done this before, but I like it when you do it."

She giggled. "I like doing it to you. Your pussy is so pink and pretty. Sammael gave you a workout, but you need more, don't you." It wasn't a question.

I nodded my head. "I need fucked."

"You fucked his fingers," she said, sliding three of her own inside me.

I groaned and arched my back, wiggling my hips so I fucked myself on her fingers. "Yes," I said. "I did. But I need more."

She slipped in a fourth finger, wiggling and twisting her hand to get as deep in me as she could. I moaned, spreading my legs wider. There was no way to resist looking up. Daemon gently helped support me while I watched her screwing her hand into my cunt.

"Stretching me..." I whimpered. "So tight. So much!"

She raised one delicate eyebrow. "Too much?"

"No!" I cried, my hand going to her wrist. I didn't want her to pull out or to stop. Instead, I pulled her to me, like I might a dildo, trying to get her deeper. "Please, Lilith! I need it so much!"

She gave me a satisfied smile. "I knew you'd be like this," she murmured. "I watched you in the mirror," she confessed. "Watched you fucking yourself with you hand. I watched as you stifled a cry as your thumb slipped past your rim and into your pretty little soaked cunt. You're a maniac," she said, pressing harder so her thumb slipped past my ring and further into my pussy. "A hot-blooded sex kitten. Just like me." She dipped her head to flutter my clit with her tongue until I shivered and cried out.

"Yes! Oh, God! Yes! Fuck me with your hand!"

"Oh, I'm gonna," she said, her voice growing husky. "Then the men are going to have a go at you. Before the day is over, you won't care about anything or anyone but us and all the pleasure we can give you. You'll be sated and sleepy and when you wake up, we'll start it over again."

"Lilith," Daemon said, a warning in his voice. "She's not ours yet."

"She will be," the woman said with confidence. "After today, she will be."

With that, she slipped the widest part of her hand inside my cunt until the opening closed around her wrist. Then she started to fuck me with it.

Never had anything been so erotic. Daemon plucked at my nipples as Lilith fisted me and continued to lick my clit. Sammael had stripped and lazily stroked his cock, a violent hunger in his eyes. That man wanted more than just my pussy. He wanted everything.

Our eyes locked gazes and he let me know without saying that he'd have me more than once before the night was over. Planting one knee on the couch beside me, he guided his cock to my lips for me to suck. I took it without hesitation. The position made swallowing him down more difficult, but I managed to take him to the root. His balls slapped against my chin as I sucked him down.

He was careful. At first. When we got a rhythm going, however, he started fucking me as hard as Daemon had. Lilith continued to fist me and lick my clit, straying occasionally to my asshole with her other hand. She rubbed the little puckered hole and circled it over and over. I pushed out once, opening the sphincter muscle slightly. Given the fact I'd already had three fingers inside me earlier, she slipped one of hers in easily before adding a second.

God, this was depraved! If I thought about it too much I was sure I'd be mortified at my own behavior... On second thought, maybe I wouldn't. It felt too good to regret it. Or to want to stop.

I hummed around Sammael's cock while Daemon continued to twist and tug my nipples. My body was coated in sweat and my face was a mess. But I didn't want it any other way. I wanted this dirty, messy, sweaty sex. The bite of pain with the pleasure was exactly what I needed. Already, I'd come more times that I could remember. I knew the monsters had given me orgasm after orgasm, but that was a haze of dream. The longer I was away from them, the less real it felt.

"That's it, beautiful pet," Daemon praised. "Swallow him down. Take all Lilith gives you. *Love it!*"

I squealed out another orgasm. I *did* love it. Every filthy second of it.

"Hey! What the fuck? You motherfuckers started without me?" It was another male. I thought I recognized the voice, but couldn't concentrate on anything other than taking the cock currently fucking my face.

"You knew when she came through the gate it wouldn't be long, Abbadon," Daemon said. "Was she followed?"

"No. No sentinels were on her. They just left her on her own."

"Good," Daemon purred. "We will have a claim. A good one if she imprints while here."

"I've never seen her like," the newcomer said. "She rivals even Lilith in beauty."

From between my legs, Lilith chuckled. "She does. A very beautiful pussycat indeed. I could just eat her up." She smirked. "Oh, wait…"

Chuckles all around.

"Is she stretched enough?" Abbadon must have been the guard at the gate. He was the only other person I'd seen here. "I want to fuck her ass."

"She's almost there," Lilith said. "But you're welcome to fuck my ass while you're waiting on our precious little kitten. Maybe it will take the edge off for you and you can enjoy her more when it's time."

Oh, God! I wanted to see that. Wanted to watch Lilith's face as he entered her ass. Would she wince or smirk? I got the feeling the latter.

"Let her up, Sammael," Daemon said. "Just for a moment. Then you can plant your cum in her throat."

Sammael let me up, growling his displeasure, but kneeling down to whisper in my ear. "Do you think she's going to love that big cock of Abbadon's in her ass?"

"Yes," I breathed. "I think she will."

Lilith gave us a cocky smirk before looking back over her shoulder. "Stop dicking around and put that cock in my ass, you pussy," she said. Abbadon's nostrils flared and he smacked her ass twice in rapid succession.

"Bitch," he muttered. "We'll see who's laughing when I destroy this tiny asshole."

"Tell me how he feels," I whispered, my gaze clinging to Lilith's as he impaled her from behind.

Her eyes widened slightly before she arched her back, raising her ass higher in offering. "Abbadon's cock always stretches me a little. He's not small. But it feels delicious." She licked her lips before dipping her head and swiping her tongue around my opening where her fist was buried deep.

"And I love it when he spanks my ass. Especially when he's fucking it too."

As if in answer to her, Abbadon smacked her ass again. "Little whore," he bit out. "Take my cock like a good whore."

"Awww," Lilith purred. "You say the sweetest things." She grinned while Abbadon bared his teeth at her. His movements were jerky and his fingers bit deep into Lilith's ass cheeks, but soon he was riding her hard and rough, fucking her asshole.

I panted watching them. The harder Abbadon fucked Lilith, the harder she fucked my pussy with her fist. I felt like Abbadon was fucking both of us and it felt *great*! I cried out once, then Sammael smacked my face with his cock, drawing my attention back to him.

"Get back here, little pet," he growled. "I need my cock down that throat."

I turned my head and opened my mouth eagerly and Sammael fisted my hair and thrust deep. I gagged once, but relaxed and tilted my head at a better angle to take him. He quickly found his rhythm and pounded into my mouth.

"That's it, pet," Daemon growled. "You look so hot like this. Lilith's fist in your little pussy. Sammael's cock down your throat." I could hear Sammael grunting and groaning as he fucked my face. Saliva leaked from the corners of my mouth but he didn't let me do more than gasp in a breath. Slimy, sweaty sex. In a flash of insight, I knew I'd always crave this kind of fucking.

Gripping my hair ever tighter, Sammael panted, grunting with every breath. "Gonna…

fuckin'… COME!" He roared his release, his hot cum spilling down my throat and into my mouth. Again, some leaked from the corners of my mouth. Sammael had to force me to let him go as I continued sucking. The second I did, Lilith was there, kissing me and swapping his cum with me. She was more aggressive this time, taking what she wanted. She rose above me slightly and let cum dribble from her mouth back to mine only to repeat the lusty kiss.

I moaned into her mouth as she held my jaw with one hand while she kissed. Me. "Filthy little kitten," she whispered. I could smell my pussy on the hand she held my face with. Felt my own moisture on my skin. "Were all gonna fuck you. By the time this day is done, you'll be ours as much as you are theirs."

It wasn't the first time she'd said this and I wasn't sure what to make of it, but if it meant I got sex day and night, why not have them both?

I looked up into her eyes. Their gorgeous depths seemed to glow as the sunlight from a nearby window caressed her face. Her skin seemed even darker and glistened with sweat. In the golden sunlight, it looked like fire dancing over her flesh.

"Ah, I see our beautiful pet is here. Did the *Masakh fi Flkhizana* require her prepared again?"

"Blazin," Daemon welcomed, beckoning to the other man. "I see you remember our pet from yesterday."

"How could I forget?" He gave me a satisfied grin. "Her pussy and ass were the best I've had in recent memory."

"The *Masakh fi Flkhizana* have not seen to her needs properly. She's here for the help she needs."

Blazin's face hardened. "What?" He bit out the question and balled his hands into fists at his side.

"She's imprinting faster than they expected. Says she was fucking herself soon after she rose this morning, needing relief. Unable to get it herself, she came to us."

"Fuck," Blazin swore. "The elders aren't going to like this."

"The laws are clearly written. If we can seduce her away from them and she imprints on us instead of them, she's ours."

"The monsters may seek revenge."

Daemon shrugged. "We're strong. I'm not worried. Besides, they should have planned better. Ensured she was indeed able to leave their realm during the day."

Blazin shook his head, but started shedding his clothing. "This is a really bad idea."

"Maybe, but she's worth it."

Chapter Four

Blazin walked to me and sighed as he looked at me and Lilith. The woman was scooting back down my body, presenting her ass in the air, back to Abbadon who smacked her ass before sliding back inside her back entrance and beginning to fuck her again.

"She's an exquisite specimen," he murmured, stroking his cock over me. His dick, like the other men's, was long and thick. His own fingers didn't close all the way around it. "I'd love to know she was just waiting for me to come fuck her." He reached down and scooped a dollop of cum from my chin and fed it back to me. "I want to fuck her sweet pussy again."

Daemon chuckled. "You can do that and more, my friend. See how willing she is?"

"You came to us of your own free will then?" He was questioning me but all I could do was nod as I panted. Abbadon had stopped fucking Lilith and she'd positioned herself so she scissored my body. Leaning forward, she wiggled her pelvis until our pussies aligned perfectly. She gasped at the same time I did and I knew she had it right. My clit had the perfect amount of friction and the pleasure she built inside me was amazing.

Then Abbadon slipped back inside her ass and started fucking her again. We were flush against each other, but each time his body struck Lilith's, the friction increased slightly. She kissed me as she continued to grind against my body, dancing on

Abbadon's cock at the same time.

"Fucking hell," Blazin hissed. "It's like she's in fucking heat! How the hell could they miss this? She had to be showing signs of imprinting before she left them."

"Their loss is our gain."

After several seconds in which Blazin seemed to think it over, he gave a curt nod. "Agreed."

As if Blazin's agreement with Daemon was a confirmation, Lilith sighed and began to grind against me in earnest. The friction was perfect. The sharp jarring of her body as Abbadon fucked her was the complement I needed to push me over the edge once again. I screamed with Lilith as we both came. Abbadon bit out a sharp, "Mother fuck!" and buried himself deep.

"Fucking bastard," Lilith bit out over her shoulder. "Fill my ass with your cum!"

He swatted her ass several times as he finally roared his release, the veins in his neck standing out in stark relief. They were both lovely in their passion. I only hoped I looked as pleased because I felt more wonderful than I'd ever thought possible. And this was only the beginning.

"That's it," Blazin praised as he lifted me from the couch into his arms. "You look so beautiful when you come." He kissed me deeply, heedless of the lingering cum on my face and lips. "But I'm betting you need more. Don't you."

"I want it all," I breathed out, my voice catching. "Why am I still horny?" Though I'd come over and over, there was still an ache deep inside me.

"Tell me what you need, my beautiful pet."

I looked back at Daemon, unsure what to say. "Just tell him what you need. What do you want him to do to you?"

"I-I want…" I took a deep breath. "I want you to use me," I practically whispered. "Use me in any way you want. For your pleasure."

Blazin raised an eyebrow. "In any way? That leaves a lot open."

"Yes," I said with a shiver. The lust inside me was still building. Without someone actively fucking me, it was building faster. "I feel like… I feel like if I don't get sex, if I can't have someone fucking me every second of every day, I'm going to explode with the pent up… *stuff* inside me!"

"That doesn't mean you need to be used as a sex toy, pet."

"But I *am* a pet," I interrupted. "I'm here to be your plaything. I know it like I know my own name. It just feels right. If that means you all need to fuck me then do it. If you need to punish me, it's OK. I'll enjoy it. Use my body for your pleasure."

Blazin nodded. "Yeah. You're our pet."

"Yes," I confirmed. "I'm your pet. To do with as you please."

He looked up at Daemon and grinned. "She's perfect." He carried me across the room and placed me on one of the fur-covered padded benches. This one had a pillory at one end and straps on the wide bench. I looked at it in anticipation rather than fear. It didn't take much of an imagination to know what this was for.

"Are you going to put me in that?"

"Do you want me to?" Blazin raised an eyebrow at me.

I wasn't sure if this was a test or not but remembered what Daemon had said at the beginning of the day. Tell the truth. I did. "Yes. Very much."

"You'd be at our mercy. Anyone we brought in here could fuck you if they wanted. You'd be powerless to stop them."

I shrugged. "If it gets me fucked, then I'm for it. Do your worst. Bring in whomever you want."

For the briefest of moments, Blazin's eyes looked like there was a flickering flame in their emerald depths. He looked pleased in the extreme. "You may regret those words, pet. Be careful."

I wiggled, trying to get down. Blazin let me and I turned around, kneeling on the bench and placing my neck and wrists in the pillory holes. The padding for my knees was plush and comfortable, allowing me to hold my weight easily. The pillory itself was padded and lined with soft fur. I lowered the thing down until it fell into place. I had to wiggle one wrist into its hole, but since it wasn't latched, it wasn't hard.

"Well, then," Blazin said. "I guess you know what you want. You're safe word is red. If it gets too rough, or you need to stop for any reason, I expect you to use that word. Do you understand me, pet?"

"Red," I repeated. "I understand."

He locked the pillory and moved to strap my legs into place. Those restraints weren't necessarily needed, but it made me feel less in control. I couldn't move at all.

"Daemon," Blazin said, raising his voice. "Do you have plans for the little pet?"

"I do. But first, we all get to fuck her. Lilith has had her turn, but I suspect she'll want more. If you need a strap-on, get it. You'll go once someone has put his cum inside her."

"Thank you, Daemon," Lilith said. Until now, it had been pretty much anything goes. Now, I felt more of a formality to everything.

"She's no longer a virgin," Daemon said, "but she's our sacrifice. She's to be our pet which means she's to be satisfied above everything else. An unhappy pet is a destructive pet." That got some chuckles all around. But hadn't I said as much the night before when the monsters had been arguing?

Daemon continued. "The rules are simple. You must be mindful of our pet at all times. Should she seem to be in discomfort, you stop and assess the situation. If you are not the one fucking her and you see she's in distress, you make it known. She's ours to play with. Not to abuse beyond what she enjoys."

"Understood, leader," they said in unison.

"Then, play. But make sure you put every single load of cum inside her body somewhere."

"Understood, leader." Again, they verbalized in unison. I was helpless. Locked in a pillory willingly. And all these men were about to use me. Oh. And Lilith. I got the feeling she wouldn't be denied.

I felt someone at my back, rubbing my ass cheeks, slapping them lightly. Then harder. When I cried out, there was as deep chuckle behind my back.

"She's so responsive," Blazin said. "Her little pussy is dripping with honey even after already being fucked. How many times has she orgasmed today?

"Not nearly enough," Daemon answered. Then he was at my head, in front of me feeding me his cock. I couldn't reach for him since my hands were in the pillory. All I could do was open my mouth and take what he gave me. The realization made me groan and I felt my pussy juice make a slow trickle down my inner thigh. Someone -- probably Blazin -- scooped it up with a fingertip.

"Mmmm... so tasty." Yeah. It was Blazin. "So wet for us."

"I am," I sighed. "Fuck me."

Daemon grabbed a handful of my hair as he fed me his cock. I opened my mouth wide, taking what he offered. As I looked up at him, I watched his eyes close as he smiled. "So fucking good," he murmured. "Gonna fuck your throat, pet."

"Mmmm," I said around his cock.

"I think she likes this," Blazin said. He sounded like he was still behind me. I thought it was his hand running down my ass to my pussy. His fingers slid inside me. "Yes. All nice and wet."

"Fuck her, brother. She's sweet and succulent," Lilith purred. She was somewhere beside me, but I couldn't tell where. "And once you come inside her, I get to fuck whichever hole your cum is in."

I whimpered around Daemon's cock as he fucked my face with it. He wasn't fucking me fast yet, but he'd worked his way deep. I knew it wouldn't be long until he fucked me hard. And I was eager for it. I could do nothing to hasten them either. All I could do was kneel there and take whatever they decided to give me.

I felt the blunt tip of a cock at my pussy and tried to push out. The restraints held firm. They must have fastened the straps on my legs to something to keep me from rocking back because I barely moved an inch.

A sinister chuckle sounded from behind me where Blazin's cock was still at the entrance to my pussy. "You can't take what we don't give you, pet," he said. "You are completely at our mercy."

Again, I whimpered in need. I wanted this. I hadn't realized how much until I was unable to encourage or entice. All I could do was stay there and await their pleasure.

Then, with one swift movement, Blazin surged forward, holding himself deep inside me for one glorious second.

Then he fucked me.

He rocked me, pounding into me with brute force. The pillory stood firm, but he bounced around me with the force of his fucking. Like before, the movements of the man at my back made the fucking my mouth was taking even more intense. I loved every second of it.

I gagged several times, but Daemon kept his cock in my mouth. Truth be told, had he tried to remove it, I might have bit down to keep it. Saliva dripped steadily from my mouth as he continued.

"Fucking little whore," he bit out. "You fucking love this, don't you." He didn't seem to expect an answer as he continued to pull my hair as he fucked me. "I'm gonna come in your mouth, and I want you to swallow every fucking drop. You hear me? Don't lose one single... drop... *AHHHH!!*" With a brutal yell, Daemon's cock exploded in my mouth. Hot, sticky cum erupted, pouring down my throat. He held himself deep, my nose pressed against the base of his cock until the spurts of seed finished. Then he pulled out and I gasped for breath I hadn't realized I desperately needed.

Almost immediately, Blazin's roar of completion rang in my ears and his cock pulsed inside me. Another load of cum flowed inside my body. Blazin gripped my ass, his nails digging into my tender flesh. His cock pulsed and throbbed inside my needy little cunt and he stayed there for a long time. I remembered how Dokkin had knotted with me the first time he'd fucked me and wondered if Blazin had done the same. But he wasn't a monster. So he couldn't. Right?

"Ready Lilith?"

"Just let me get positioned below you so your cum doesn't drip out," she said. Then I felt the cool touch of latex as she eased inside when Blazin withdrew. "There," she purred, rubbing a gentle hand down the length of my back before gripping my hips. "Such a pretty little pussycat. Such a needy little pet."

I gasped, wanting so much to look over my shoulder at her darkly beautiful face. With my pale skin and her dark skin, I bet we made a beautiful sight.

"That's it, Lilith," Abbadon said. "Fuck her. Make her come. Then I'm taking her tight little ass."

"Just wait your turn," Lilith said with a chuckle. "She's primed for as much as we want to give her."

"She's definitely the horniest pet we've ever had. To be able to keep up with all of us, she'd have to be." Sammael commented.

"So lovely... I want to suck her tits." That was Daemon again. Then he slid underneath me and took one of my nipples into his mouth. "Mmmm," he hummed around my tit. "She's perfect."

There were murmurs of agreement all around me. Then I could only concentrate on the pleasure building inside me. The dildo Lilith was using was long and thick. It stretched and burned but in a way that made me mad with lust. The need to come.

I screamed as she found my clit with a finger and flicked. Cum exploded from me, both Blazin's and my own. I felt it. When Lilith praised me as she fucked me harder, I knew I had definitely squirted.

"My, oh my, what a lusty creature," she chuckled. "I'm definitely going to have fun with you, my pretty little pussycat." Then she spanked my clit with the flat of her fingers. Once. Then again. Harder. Over and over she did this while she kept up the rhythm of the strap-on fucking my cunt. I cried out with each hit until the pleasure finally overtook the pain and I came again with a scream so hard it made my throat raw. My vision blurred and I would have collapsed had it not been for the restraints holding me up.

The next thing I knew, Abbadon was cramming his dick in my ass, squirting lube as he did. He was thick and long. I wasn't sure he'd fit, but it didn't take much before I felt his abdomen against my ass.

"Now, little pet. I fuck you."

And, boy, did he ever. Abbadon pounded into me like a jackhammer, deep, rapid thrusts I had no hope of keeping up with.

Sammael stood in front of me, stroking his cock. "That's it, pet. Do you like his rough fucking?"

"Yesss!" I screamed the word on a keening wail as I came yet again. "Fuck my ass! Oh, God!"

"You like your ass fucking?" Abbadon gasped out. "Fuckin' little hole is fuckin' strangling my fuckin' dick!"

"Yes! Yes! Fuck my ass, you bastard!"

"FUCK!" Abbadon kept moving, surging into me like he was trying to destroy my ass. But I thrived on it. Reveled in it! The more he gave me, the better I liked it. The more I needed it.

"Fuck me harder! Faster!"

"Fuck me," Sammael hissed. "She's wild. Beyond control."

"I thought she might be," Daemon said, softly. As if he were confiding in Sammael about a problem he had. "It's why I put her in the pillory. We can control her movements and she doesn't get hurt."

"I'm not sure we have to worry about that, brother," Sammael said.

"What do you mean?" Daemon barked. I could barely follow the thread of the conversation, but I was sure it was important.

"I think she may be a latent succubus. It explains how she could be a virgin and still take everything we or the monsters give her."

There was a long silence. Then, "Impossible. We'd have been informed."

"Not impossible. The *Masakh fi Flkhizana* had claimed her as the *muluk alhayawanat al'alifa*. The King's Pet. Even if she is a succubus, their claim would supersede ours."

"Do you think they realized what she was?"

"I doubt it. If they had, they'd have never let us take her virginity. It also explains why she came back to us instead of waiting in the closet close to her monsters."

"Then, this isn't an imprinting. It's a feeding."

"Exactly." Sammael didn't sound worried. In fact, he sounded satisfied. Immensely satisfied.

"We'll have to get her tested, but if you're right, she'll recuperate quickly and be fucking one or more of us a couple of hours after this session." Daemon continued to think through the new development. "The five of us can't hope to keep a succubus."

"We'll work it out," Sammael said, then moved away.

I felt a cock at my pussy then. Abbadon paused to adjust his stance, presumably further up my body to allow room for the newcomer.

"Now, little pet," Sammael purred. "You're going to be filled with cum in your little ass, and this sweet, sweet cunt. When you do, you're going to come with us. Do you understand?"

"Yes," I gasped. "I'll come when you come."

And they fucked me.

Lilith was soon in front of me, kissing me passionately, licking the insides of my mouth with her delicate tongue. "Does it feel good to have two cocks inside you?" Between kisses, Lilith stoked my lusts.

"It does," I gasped.

"Pretty, needy little pet. You love having the men fuck you, don't you."

"I do!"

"Can you take more? I bet you can."

As she spoke, hand undid the restraints on my thighs. Lilith helped remove the pillory. Then Blazin slid under me, pulling me down to him. With practiced movements, he maneuvered his cock so that he slipped in beside Sammael inside my pussy.

I cried out. I was so stuffed, it was hard to breathe. But Blazin kissed me and found my nipples with his fingers. He pulled and tugged until I relaxed and began moving with them again.

"That's my sweet pet," he whispered. "You can take us."

Chapter Five

I turned my head and Daemon was beside me, his cock bobbing beside my face. Without thinking, I grabbed it, pulling him to my mouth to suck on. His head fell back on a groan as I pulled greedily. "Lusty wench," he growled. "My needy little succubus."

I didn't know what that meant or why he and Sammael thought I was one, but I didn't really care. If it got me this much pleasure, who cared? I was lost in this world of sensation and raunchy pleasure, and I couldn't be happier.

Lilith knelt beside me, stroking damp hair out of my face as I continued to suck on Daemon. "That's it, baby," she crooned. "You look so lovely with Daemon's cock in your mouth." She kissed my eyelids. Then my nose. Then she placed her lips on Daemon's cock beside mine and slid up and down his shaft with me. "Mmmm…" she moaned around it as Daemon began to take control of the pace.

I just opened my mouth and let him fuck me, closing my lips around him when I could, relaxing when I couldn't. Lilith did much the same, only she stayed beside me, her luscious lips sucking him from the side.

"The two of you look so damned dirty," he said, his voice strained and his movements erratic. "So fucking hot!" With a groan, he spilled his seed inside my mouth. I didn't swallow, knowing Lilith would want her share too. He pulled out, his cock still spurting cum. The second he did, Lilith fused her mouth to mine, licking inside, taking his cum from me only to spit it down. I licked it from her chin and kissed her again, over and over until we drank every drop. All the while, Daemon continued to spurt over our faces. When he was done, we licked and cleaned each other while Abbadon, Sammael, and Blazin continued to fuck me.

It wasn't long before I felt all three of the remaining men inside me swell. I whimpered as I continued to kiss Lilith, needing their cum inside me in the worst way. I felt like I'd die without it.

"Don't worry, my lovely pet," Lilith said between kisses. "They'll fill you full." She kissed me one last time then stood before me. "Lick my pussy, little pet."

I did. Without hesitation. She spread her legs and tilted her pelvis while I latched onto her clit with my lips and sucked. On impulse, I slid my fingers inside her, pumping her pussy with them. "Mmmm…" I moaned, licking and sucking. I scooped out her juice and licked my fingers, then wrapped my arm around her body, pulling her close to me.

Better able to get my mouth over her cunt, I lapped at her opening, greedy for that sweet nectar she produced. "I love the way you taste," I gasped out as the men fucked me harder and harder. The snarls and swearing coming from behind me told me they had to be close. "I'd love to lick their cum out of you like you did me."

"You'll get your chance," Daemon said. He stood before me, glistening in sweat from his own exertion. With his cock still hard, the veins prominent all over it, he looked like some kind of dark god. Or a fallen angel. Or maybe a risen demon.

I looked up at him, holding his gaze while the other three men pounded me from behind and beneath. We held each other's gaze for long, long moments. Then finally, Daemon grinned down at me, a predatory grin. A carnivorous grin. "Come, my beauty. Come for me and make them come with you."

It was like he'd flipped some kind of switch inside me. The second the words were out of his mouth, my orgasm hit me with an explosive force nothing short of nuclear. I screamed over and over, my body convulsing hard.

Dimly, I heard the men around me shout out their own releases. Felt them release inside me. Felt their cum leak from my body with they pulled out of me. But my orgasm went on and on until I finally collapsed in a whimpering, quivering heap.

The next thing I remember was being in Daemon's arms as he sat with me in a hot tub. The water bubbled and fizzed around us, heating my skin. Making me horny all over again.

"What's happening to me?" I asked, my voice quivering. I was beginning to be really frightened now. "Why am I like this?"

"I don't know, pet, but we'll figure it out."

"What's a succubus?"

Daemon paused for a moment, then sighed. "A succubus is a demon halfling that takes nourishment from sex. Both the sexual energy of an orgasm, and the physical form of cum from either a male or female can feed a succubus."

"But... I'm human."

"We thought so, too. Even the monsters did. Now, I'm not so sure."

"How do we find out?"

"You'll have to go before the council of demons."

"What about the monsters?" I was worried they'd be deprived of their prize. I was mad at them for leaving me in such a condition, but I still kind of liked them. Besides, it sounded like they had no reason to believe they were leaving me in such bad shape.

"I don't know, pet. It's hard to say. They left you, but they also likely had no idea what you are. At least, what I *think* you are."

Even though the bubbles in the hot tub were stimulating me, I could feel an overwhelming lethargy beginning to overtake me. My eyelids drooped and I struggled to stay awake. "I'm sleepy," I said, my voice small and tired.

"Yes. Figured as much." Daemon gave my body a cursory going over, washing the cum and sweat from my skin. Then he lifted me out and dried me before carrying me to a massive bed in another room.

He laid me in the bed, then crawled in behind me, wrapping me up in his arms so my head was pillowed on his arm and his body was tucked in securely behind me. "Sleep, little pet. You'll be safe with me. When you wake, we'll figure out our next move."

I nodded, already falling asleep. I had no idea what would happen when I woke, but I had the feeling whatever it was, I'd be more than ready for it. For now, though. I'd just lay still in Daemon's arms and... *Sleep*.

Monster In My Closet Mates A Succubus
(Monster World 3)
A Razor's Edge Monster Erotica Short
Wanda Violet O.

It's been one hell of a day. First, I met the monster in my closet. He demanded I lose my virginity before he came for me last night. I'm new to this world, but I know I've somehow changed, and my life will never be the same. Something is happening. I'm stronger than anyone I know. I may be a pet, but if left on her own, this pet gets destructive...

WARNING: This is a short monster erotica novella... if you want a strong plot and character development, you won't find them here. What you will find is hot sex and one satisfied woman -- with a monster out of the closet and in her bed... along with a few other beings.

Chapter One

Sunlight bathed my naked body in warmth. I lay in a bed of soft furs and pillows, surrounded by naked men. A naked woman sprawled next to me, her hand gripping my right tit possessively. All of them were sound asleep. All but one.

Daemon stood at the window, looking out into the sunset. He leaned against the wall, arms crossed over his massive chest. His buttocks were rounded and muscled, making me want to crawl to him on my hands and knees and lick all that delicious flesh while working my way between his legs to start on his cock.

It had truly been one hell of a day. First, I met the monster in my closet. He demanded I lose my virginity before he came for me last night. Which is when I first met Daemon. He'd been the first one to fuck me. Him and several of his friends. I'd never felt so good -- or so exhilarated. They'd taken me in a club, on the dance floor. Fucked me there for all to see. There were bodies pressing all around us, the lights pulsing and strobing. They were writhing against one another as much as Daemon and I. The only thing was, Daemon had friends. Together, they'd shown me one hell of a time. It had awakened something in me. Something dark and maybe even a little bit dangerous. It had also prepared me for the monster in my closet. Or rather, monsters.

When I'd gotten home, the monster had taken me to his realm. Fucked me. Then given me to his brothers and we'd all had a fucking party. Literally.

They'd taken me over and over, filling me with their cum. Most of them had at least attempted to be gentle. I hadn't wanted gentle. Still didn't. I pushed them as much as they pushed me.

Then they'd left me. Left me to fend for myself. They said something about an imprinting or something. I got the impression that they thought I'd eventually cling to them, that I'd need them in some way. That the imprinting would make me need them sexually every hour of every day. I thought they were right. Except instead of it being a gradual process, it started hours later.

When I woke up early that morning, I was hornier than I ever imagined a person could be. I was *insane* for sex. I'd remembered Dokkin, the head monster, telling me to seek out Daemon if my cravings got to be too much. Turns out Daemon was keeping an eye on me. He knew the situation I was in, knew I had no hope of making it until the monsters came for me. At least, I *think* that's what happened. He called me, offering to ease my suffering if I came to him.

Which is where my morning orgy came in. Four men and a woman. Looking back now, I'm certain they're demons. They may serve the monsters in my closet, but they are monsters in their own right. But even they were no match for my sexual appetite. They thought they were; there were five of them and one of me. I might have slept, but I woke up energized. Horny, and energized. I had the feeling this was only the beginning. I'd outlasted them all and could happily go back for more. They were all passed out. Worn out and drained of energy.

Well, all of them but Daemon. He was calculating. Like he knew he'd missed something. I'd heard him talking with Blazin, his apparent second in command, when the party had really taken off. He seemed to think I'm a succubus. Whatever that is. They said something about taking me before the demon council but I kind of lost the thread after that.

Now, with everyone else passed out in the big fur bed I'd woken up in, I found myself alone with Daemon.

As if he felt my eyes devouring him, Daemon turned his head to find me staring at him. He smiled and beckoned to me to come to him. The others didn't move as I maneuvered my way off the fur bed. They'd all been magnificent that morning, fucking me until we'd all finally passed out. All but Daemon.

"What's wrong?" He pulled me into his arms. It was an affectionate gesture, but one I sensed he thought he should do rather than something he felt. A stall tactic, maybe?

"How do you feel, Wyn? Do you hurt?"

"Not at all, Daemon." I frowned, thinking about my answer. "After all I've been through in the last twenty-four hours, I should be sore as hell, but I'm not." I looked up at him. He didn't seem surprised, just contemplative. "What is it?"

"We'll have company tonight," he said softly. "They'll want to... talk to you."

"I can't. I have to get back home. The monsters are supposed to come for me."

"Not before you meet with my clan." The look Daemon gave me wasn't unkind, but it was firm.

"But, why? You were supposed to help me until it was time for the monsters to come back for me. I'm supposed be theirs."

"Maybe." He smiled at me, reaching out to brush a finger down my cheek. "Maybe not."

Slowly, he bent his head to mine and took my lips in a kiss. The contact seemed to ignite something inside me like a firestorm. I groaned as I deepened the kiss, trying to devour him. I found his cock with my hand, stroking as I rubbed by body against his in desperate need.

"Need to fuck you," I whimpered. "Need it now, Daemon."

"Little fucking bitch." He grabbed a fist full of my hair and shoved me to my knees. I didn't wait for any instructions. Instead, I gripped his hips and wrapped my mouth around his cock. I swallowed him down greedily, humming with every pull. He bit out a strangled yell, throwing his head back. The muscles in his arms and chest stood out in stark relief. Then I felt his other hand in my hair. He had two fistfuls, trying to guide me, trying to slow my movements.

Fuck that shit.

I dug my nails into his ass and took him as deep as I could, swallowing his cock. Over and over I swallowed, massaging the head, taking the drops of precum he spilled because of my efforts. It was mine by right. I wanted it all!

"Fuck! Fuck!"

"Mmmm…"

I took him as deep as I could. My face was against his abdomen now, the considerable length of him down my fucking throat. He throbbed in the confined space, against my walls. I gagged but it only let me take him that much deeper. Then I swallowed once more.

Daemon roared, coming in a flood. I swallowed greedily, energy flowing through my body like I'd mainlined a week's worth of caffeine.

When his pleasure seemed to crest, the spurts of his cock decreasing in strength, I tunneled my finger between his cheeks to find his asshole. Pressing against his back entrance, I sank my finger inside, finding his prostate unerringly. A few flicks and he was coming again.

Sweat broke out over Daemon's body. His hands shook in my hair and his body trembled as he came and came. I drank him down, power filling me like I'd never imagined. Sexual power. The power of a woman over a man. He'd thought he could master me, but he wasn't man enough. Looking up into his face, that helpless expression looking down at me as I took every single inch he had to give me, I could tell Daemon knew it, too.

Over and over I brought Daemon to the edge of madness. Over and over I shoved him over. Every time he came, every time I swallowed his cum, I grew more and more powerful. It frightened me but I embraced it.

With a hoarse cry, Daemon came one more, soul shattering time, then fell to his knees. His cock was still hard, but the big demon had given me all he could, his body giving out.

I turned my head to look where I knew the others now watched. All four of them watched with wide, unbelieving eyes.

"You are a succubus," Blazin murmured. "Is he dead?"

I shrugged. "He gave me all he could. I don't think he's dead. Just needs to recover." I thought I sounded like I was in a daze. It felt like I was high, but hyperaware of my surroundings. I knew others approached. Many. Maybe thirty of them. All male. "They're coming." I said, looking at Blazin. "For me?"

"Yes, little pet. They want to test you."

"What for?"

"To see if you're truly a succubus." He looked wary, like he wasn't sure what he was hoping for.

"And if I am?"

"We'll argue your monsters didn't take care of your needs. That they abused you by leaving a succubus alone without sustenance during her transition."

I tilted my heat, trying to make sense of what he was saying. "What do you get out of it? Daemon is the strongest of you and he couldn't master me. What makes you think you can?"

Blazin looked at Abbadon. "It wouldn't be just us, though once your transition is complete we intend to be your keepers."

"But you have to survive the transition…"

I thought for a moment. The demons were approaching. Many demons. I couldn't see them, but I could sense them. "You hope the horde of demons coming to "interview" me will be able to give me what I need to transition."

"Yes." Sammael, the cordial one, the one who had soothed me this morning when he was afraid things would get too rough, stepped forward. Trying to smooth the way most likely. "You need guidance and stout males in their prime ready to give you the sexual energy your kind crave." He reached out a hand to me, trying to get me to go to him. Everything in me was telling me not to. Not yet. His time would come, but not yet.

"And what do you get out of it?"

"A transitioning succubus." That voice. Joy filled my heart.

"Dokkin?" I whispered his name, my instinct telling me to go to him, but something held me back.

"She's ours," Blazin said sharply. "You abandoned her in her greatest time of need."

"No, we didn't," Mikkos snapped. "We left her to push her need to the fore. The more she lets that need build, the more easily she is to guide."

"You mean control," I retorted. "I'm not your plaything."

"Yes, you are," Fukkon said. *That* hurt the most. I remember feeling like Dokkin was my protector, but Fukkon was the one who saw the real me. At least, I'd built that fantasy. "You're ours to pleasure. Ours to play with. Our reward for centuries of work for the kingdom of monsters. But you're also ours to please. Protect. Our greatest treasure."

Chapter Two

"I'm more than that." I wanted to be anyway.

Dokkin nodded. "I can see that's who you are, Wyn. If you truly want to be our equal, then you need to meet with the Council of Demons. Just understand they will indeed test you. If you can take their lusts and bring them to their knees" -- he nodded toward Daemon where he lay crumpled in a heap on the floor -- "you'll walk away as one of the most powerful succubi in the realm."

"And if I can't?"

"You lose your power and strength. A succubus's transition can follow one of two paths. Slow and gradual, or explosive. The slow transition might take you months or even years, but, once you've shed your human self, you'd feed only on sexual energy and cum. The rapid transformation gains you more power, but it's dangerously hard for a human to make that kind of transition. And a human wouldn't survive being our pet for long, Wyn. You have to know that."

I wanted to cry. "Why didn't you just tell me all of this? I'd have done my best to hold out and wait for you."

"Would you?" Fukkon asked. "Knowing that by letting your desire build, we were trying to better control you?"

I couldn't answer that question. "You still should have told me."

"Yes," Dokkin acknowledged. "But now you have to make a choice. Challenge the demon horde, or come back with us."

"You should know that the process has already started," Sivvour said. "You're going to be a whore no matter what. What the demons have started might not be slowed down, so you're going to want to fuck everything in sight."

"Wow, Sivvour," I said mockingly. "I'm going to be a whore no matter what?"

"Well, yeah," he said with a shrug. "You're going to have to fuck an entire horde of demons to make it through this. Even that might not be enough."

"That doesn't make me a whore, you asshole. It makes me a fighter! So I'll tell you what. You bring on the fucking horde of demons. I'll put them all on their knees like I did Daemon. When I'm done, I'll come for the five of you..." I trailed off, looking around the room. "Where's Bob?"

Mikkos hiked a thumb over his shoulder. "Out with the demons. Apparently, he's drinking buddies with some of them. Not sure if he's trying to call them off or give them pointers."

I took a breath, trying to calm myself. When I opened my eyes, I stared down Sivvour. "I will break you. Make you beg me to let you fuck me then make you watch as every single one of your brothers gets all the pleasure they can stand. Then I'll take my pleasure in denying you any part of my body."

Sivvour just smirked. "Right. Let me know how that works out for you."

"You're our prize." Mikkos waved his hand dismissively. "You're here for our pleasure. Not the other way around."

I nodded slowly, moving my gaze to the other man. "We'll see about that."

It was amazing the difference a day could make. Last night I'd been in awe of these men. I'd craved their attentions. The pleasure they all gave me. I could have happily lived like that for the rest of my days. I'd been a plaything to them. Their "reward for all the great shit they'd done for all monster kind or some shit. Now, something was different inside me. The power dynamic had somehow shifted. I wasn't completely in charge and I wasn't sure I could take all of them, but I could -- and would -- pick my battles carefully. Unless the others banded together and forced me, I vowed that, no matter how many men I fucked tonight, Mikkos and Sivvour would not be among them.

"Di'ja'll find'er?" Bob entered the room, his massive body dwarfing everyone else. Behind him were several men I assumed were demons, though they looked much like Daemon and the others. Like very large human men. They all looked at me in a calculating manor. Sizing me up? I could tell by the look on the faces of the ones closest to me they didn't think very much of me. Well, other than as a woman they wanted to fuck in the worst way.

"Yeah, Bob," Dokkin said with a sigh. "We found her." Dokkin didn't like the hillbilly accent Bob had adopted, nor did he much approve of his name, but Bob was quite possibly the only one of the bunch who would understand my need to be more than simply a plaything for them. He understood about not conforming to the expectation of others.

Bob looked at me, then to Sivvour. "He pissed

her off. Didn't he."

"Yeah. He did."

"Figured." Bob just shook his head. "Boy, you ain't got no idea what you just done, do ya?"

"Never mind that." Dokkin waved him off. Did he not think I could follow through with my threat, or was he just trying to bring Bob back to the matter at hand? "What about the Council of Demons?"

Bob shrugged. "They don't think she's no succubus. But they're willin' to hear out Daemon's clan if it means they get to fuck the little beauty." He chuckled. "Personally, I can't wait for this. Our little prize is gonna knock their balls off."

"This is why I like Bob better than any of you," I said. "Y'all can go fuck yourselves."

"Now, wait a minute," Fukkon said, taking a step forward. "I didn't do anything. Don't lump me in with these assholes."

"You didn't take up for me, either." I jumped on that right away. "If I had my way, I'd cut all of you off except Bob." My body was throbbing, but not with unbearable need. With power from the sexual energy I'd taken from Daemon. "While I'm pretty sure I'm going to get my fill, I can tell I'll need at least two of you. Bob, for sure, is getting lucky tonight." Bob grinned and rubbed his hands together like a kid. "How many of the rest of you get to fuck me depends on two things. How full I get and how much you grovel." I gave them all what I hoped was a death stare. "Fukkon, you'll be after Bob, if I have room. Then Dokkin, if I'm feeling generous. Mikkos and Sivvour are only if I have to have just that little bit more to complete this transition or whatever it is."

"Are you saying you'd deny your masters?" Dokkin narrowed his eyes at me while Bob chuckled.

"You're diggin' your own grave, Dokkin. Best you shut the fuck up and let her do her thing."

"I'm absolutely saying I'll deny you. And you're not my masters. You gave up that right when you decided to leave me on my own so you could better control me when you came for me later." When he opened his mouth to say something, I cut him off. "I'd like to know that the men I'm meant to spend the rest of my life with would defend me. Protect me. Treat me like a fucking princess!" I sniffled, emotion spiking when I didn't want it to. "Bastard." Swiping my fingers over my eyes, I glared at Dokkin. "You know what? For making me cry, you don't get anything. So fuck you."

I intended to push past Bob, but he pulled me into his arms and held me close. My face was buried solidly in his abdomen until he lifted me with an arm at my back and one under my knees. I buried my face in his neck then and just sobbed.

"I'll take care of you, little pet."

"I'm not a fucking pet!"

"Yes, you are. But, like you told us before, you can be a destructive kind of pet. Just means I'll have to give you what you want."

"We all will," Dokkin said. "All of us."

"You can all go fuck yourselves."

"Yeah, you said that." Dokkin scrubbed a hand over his face. The more agitated he was, the more monstrous he became. Already fur was trying to cover his skin, but he seemed to fight it off. They all were. Well, except Bob. He seemed more in control than the others. The demons behind us muttered to themselves. Unlike Daemon and the others, these demons looked the part. Big and muscled, their skin varied in color from red to green to onyx. All of them had horns; some short, some long and curling.

"Thought this was an inquisition, Bob." The biggest of the demons approached us. He didn't look angry or put out, just anxious. "We gonna fuck her or not?"

"Up to her," Bob said. "She only does what she wants."

"Put me down," I said, wiping my face. "What do I have to do?" I was going to do this, but I had questions. "If I really am a succubus, I want to know what it means."

"It means, little pet," Bob said with a grin -- was everything a joke to this guy? Oh wait! This was Bob The monster who'd named himself Bob. Of course, everything was a fucking joke to him! "Once you're fully transitioned, we'll be your pets."

"Bob," Dokkin hissed.

"You'll be *my* pets," I mused. "Like, under my control?"

Bob shrugged. "Not exactly. But when you'll demand sex. Often. Sometimes hourly. We've already claimed you, so if you transition the way you're meant to, you'll control us as much as we control you. You'll be stronger and more able to take our demonic lusts, which is a plus."

"How will I control you?"

Bob glanced at Dokkin and grinned. "Succubi emit a drug when they're horny. It makes their prey crave them. They'll give the succubus anything she wants. When she comes, the prey get energy. If the prey is an asshole and doesn't see to her pleasure? Well." Bob waved his hand to Daemon still laying on the floor, passed out. "You'll demand we fuck you, but we'll have to keep you satisfied if we want to live."

"And if you refuse to fuck me? Refuse to let me pleasure you?"

That seemed to give the big monster pause. He glanced at Dokkin again. This time, I saw a question in his eyes.

"Then we both die," Dokkin supplied.

"Yeah? How?" I demanded.

"You, from lack of substance. Us, because a succubus takes her mates with her when she dies from starvation."

I cocked my head. "Well. I guess that puts you all in a pickle, huh."

Bob grinned. "I knew I liked you. Yeah. That puts us in a pickle. Me? I intend to keep you as happy and full as I can."

"We don't know she is a succubus yet," one of the demons pointed out. "You know it will take all of us to push her through the transition if she is."

"And if she isn't, you could kill her," Dokkin snapped. "I'm not allowing this."

I snorted, turning to him and looking into his eyes. What I saw made me smile. "You're afraid."

"We just found you, Wyn. I don't want to lose you."

"No." I shook my head. "I mean, yeah, I don't think you want to lose me. But I think you're more afraid I'll be leading you around by your cock."

Dokkin rolled his eyes. "Believe what you want."

"Oh, I will. In fact, I think I'm going to have to insist I let the demons test this theory."

"And if you are? The demons make a play for you."

I shrugged. "Well, then, I'll guess you'll just have to prove why you should be the ones to have me."

"You're supposed to be our reward," Dokkin muttered. He actually looked like he was sulking. "We've already proven we should be the ones to have you."

"Maybe to someone else. But not to me. Now, is there anything any of you have to say to me before we start this?"

Bob grinned. "Yeah. Have a hell of a time, little pet."

Chapter Three

Bob bent to kiss my lips. It started out soft, then morphed to something hot and erotic. He flicked his tongue against mine, moved his hand between my legs to grip my pussy possessively. I was already damp, but I knew moisture wept from my cunt to wet his hand. "I'm going to be the one to finish you." He lifted his head and roared. It was such a change from my easygoing Bob, I jumped. "Her transition is mine!" He declared his intention for everyone present. "She will belong to my monster clan, but I will share her power and her pleasure."

"My power is mine," I said. "But I'll gladly gift you with any pleasure you desire."

Bob winked. "That's my girl."

"Sneaky son of a bitch," Dokkin muttered, but he was grinning. Then he raised his voice. "Let it be known, the succubus chooses to keep her power. She will be an entity unto herself. She'll share power with no one, thus making her protectors keepers of the heart. Not for her power alone."

Bob looked smug. He'd baited me into that. I still didn't get it all, but Rome wasn't built in a day. I'd figure it out. Right now, my brain wasn't in the mood for that.

"Later, you and me are gonna have a talk, Bob. Right now, though, let's get this show on the road." He just grinned at me, taking his cock out and stroking it lazily.

The demon horde moved forward.

Surprisingly, the large demons weren't pushing to the front of the group. In fact, most of them were pushing the smaller ones ahead of them. A group of six surrounded me quickly enough, cocks in hand, stroking themselves. I sank to my knees and took one between my lips, sucking the head as I pumped another one with my hand. Growls and snarls sounded around us as I rolled my eyes in bliss when I coaxed a drop of precum from the demon's dick.

"Mmmm…" I hummed around him, sinking him further into my mouth. He was wide and stretched my mouth but I kept working until I got him to the back of my throat. Like I'd done with Daemon, I swallowed him, the muscles of my throat squeezing him until he roared and gripped my head in his demonic hands. This guy was black in color, a deep ebony. His eyes were yellow as I looked up at him. He snarled and his teeth looked wicked. His horns stood up from his head and looked wicked sharp.

"Fuck!" The guy shouted as his hands bit into my scalp. It took surprisingly little effort to make his cum explode down my throat. Once he did, I kept sucking and swallowing. I gripped his ass with my free hand while I squeezed the cock of the demon standing next to him when the guy would have backed away. I shifted my gaze to him and winked.

Two more swallows, and the first demon came again. Naturally, I was going to measure these guys by Daemon since I'd really liked the man (hadn't known he was a demon at the time.) And this guy fell way short of the mark. After his third orgasm his eyes rolled back in his head and he passed out cold.

Before the other demon could back away, I engulfed his cock in my mouth, swallowing him down as well. I bobbed my head over and over, sucking him as I gripped his ass with both my hands. There were murmurs as someone dragged the first demon away but no one left the circle.

"She's powerful," someone muttered.

"Fuck that. Did you see how she worked Amon over? It'll be worth it if she drains me to experience that kind of pleasure. Maybe if I sixty-nine her... That way she gets her pleasure too."

"Good idea."

I was almost too far into it to really care what anyone was saying, but I honestly didn't want to hurt anyone. Daemon had deserved it because he'd pretended to care about me when it was really all about what power he could have if he made me his. Or his clan's.

Then the guy I was sucking came with a howl and a warm gush. I swallowed him greedily, triggering another orgasm from him. This time, instead of falling to the ground unconscious like Daemon and the other demon had, this demon kept howling, his muscles bulging and straining. His dick gave me one last spurt of cum, then he evaporated in a puff of smoke.

I gasped, sitting back on my heels. I knew that demon was dead. Or gone. Or whatever happened to demons at the end of their life span. I expected that would be the end of all this, but after a brief silence, a deafening roar of eagerness went up from the horde. Several more demons came forward, eager for their taste of me when they should be backing away, giving the succubus who'd just killed one of their number a wide berth.

"What happened?" I asked as I looked up at Bob, then back at Dokkin.

"They weren't seeing to your pleasure." Dokkin shook his head. "You can't be selfish with a succubus. I'm surprised Daemon lived through the experience. I doubt he would have had you not already been seen to earlier in the day, and had he not been a strong demon."

Before I could question him further, I was picked up and laid on top of another demon. His cock stood up in front of my face and I focused on it. I took him down greedily, sinking my mouth as far as I could. This time, I felt the demon's tongue probing my pussy with long, slow licks. I gave a muffled cry around a mouthful of cock. I thought I heard Bob chuckling but couldn't really focus on it. Instead, I simply closed my eyes and let the sensations take me over.

The demon's cock pulsed in my mouth, precum leaking more and more frequently until he exploded at the same time his tongue pushed me over the edge into my own powerful orgasm. I screamed around his dick, my body getting damp with sweat. I swallowed the cum he gave me, sucking and pulling for more. Craving the delicious taste and feel of his essence spilling inside of me.

With a cry, the demon came again. He shoved his fingers inside my pussy, pushing desperately to get me off. This time I could actually feel his life's essence pouring inside my body with his cum. It was like a mystical vibration sliding down my throat to fan out inside my entire body. The exhilaration of it made me gasp, my body tightening into another orgasm which seemed to double the exhilaration. It also settled something inside me and I understood what Dokkin meant. When I took an orgasm from the demon, I'd taken his power, his energy, and added it to myself. When he made me come, he'd received some of that energy back. Life energy. In that moment, I understood what it meant to be a succubus, the power I held over any sexual partner I took from here on out.

Maybe it was wrong, but I grinned evilly, glancing over at Dokkin, then to Sivvour. The latter swallowed and backed up a step. Bob laughed until he fell over.

Dokkin moved to my side where the demon still tongued me, grunting and snarling between my legs. "Now you understand the power of the succubus."

"I understand you're afraid of what I can do if not controlled," I said between licks of the demon's cock. Dokkin looked frustrated. Like I'd completely misunderstood what he was trying to convey.

"I tried to tell the hardheaded son of a bitch," Bob said, still chuckling and wiping tears from his eyes. "You don't control a woman of *any* species. You embrace her for who she is and celebrate what she'd capable of. And, above all, you keep her happy. You manage all that, she might not kill you." He winked at me.

"It's the 'might not kill you' part I worry about," Sivvour grumbled.

That seemed to delight Bob even more.

"Always knew you was a fuckin' pussy. It's the 'might not kill you' part that's fun. I mean, really. Where's the fun with a mate if there's not a risk of dyin'?"

Dokkin grunted, his eyes never wavering from mine as I continued to suck the cock of the demon beneath me. This time, when our orgasms hit, I was better able to accept what was happening and surrendered to it. I kept my gaze focused on Dokkin, letting him see the pleasure I was getting. Letting him know I was looking forward to the rest of the demon horde.

I thought he'd be angry or jealous or... something. Instead, he took out his cock and stroked. Like I was going to let him fuck me. Fuck them all! Bob, I'd go to willingly. Eagerly, even. I understood why he'd left them in the first Goddamned place. Then I came again and just let the demons have me.

When the demon beneath me went limp, I was picked up and straddled another demon. He lay on the floor, his cock thick and long. He urged me to rise up so he could tuck his cock beneath me before sliding it inside my pussy. His girth was daunting, but I took it. My pussy was wet and aching, welcoming the invasion. The burn as he stretched me was almost a relief and I sighed happily.

As the demon started fucking me, bouncing me up and down, another demon fed me his cock.

"Careful," one guy said. "Make sure she comes before you do." Chuckles all around.

Soon, the demon was fucking me hard and fast. Our skin slapped together loudly even over the din of the males around us. The demon feeding me his cock gripped my hair, holding me still while he fucked my mouth with increasing effort. It didn't take long for me to come, screaming around his cock. Both demons followed me, one deep in my pussy, one down my throat. The roars of the horde were deafening. Neither demon vanished in smoke, so I called it a win.

Two more demons positioned themselves. One big red demon tossed a tube of lubricant to another demon behind me, and when I sank onto the cock of the demon below me, I felt a large finger probe my ass with the cool lube. Then a stream of the stuff trickled between my cheeks, wetting everything. Not that I needed it at this point, but looking over the horde still waiting, I admitted it was a great idea.

Then I was being fed another cock, this one from a large green demon. His muscles bunched and rippled as he worked my cock into my mouth. He knelt on one knee, his other knee spread wide. I had one hand on the chest of the demon beneath me, the other under the second demon's thigh, digging my nails into his ass as I sucked him greedily.

Saliva dripped steadily from my chin, but I ignored it. The longer I sucked, the more forceful the demon became. He growled and grunted and cried out sharply. All the while, the other two demons continued to work themselves inside my tight body.

Pleasure hummed through me, but the balance was out of proportion again. The demon I sucked soon began to snap his hips against me. Hard. I tried to push him back, to let him know he'd better back off, but, apparently, he was already too far gone.

With an intense, brutal roar, he erupted cum down my throat, pulling me in deep while he gave me everything he had. Literally.

I swallowed, my throat coaxing him to give me just that little bit more. It was a completely involuntary reaction at this point. My body just took over. The next thing I knew, the dick in my mouth faded, leaving me empty and the demon gone in a puff of gray smoke.

"She's gonna decimate the horde," one of them muttered.

Another one chuckled. "Well, any dumbass who takes his pleasure before a succubus -- especially after visual proof of what happens when he does so -- is a dumbass the horde doesn't need. I say it's a great way to cull the idiots."

I had no idea who spoke, but if the demons weren't concerned I'd killed more than one of them, why the fuck should I be?

The demon at my back worked his cock inside me, apparently not bothered by the loss of a comrade. When I arched my back and rocked my hips at him he swatted my ass. Hard.

"Oh, no, little succubus," he growled, his voice deep and guttural. "You ain't makin' me come a'for you."

"Now you're gettin' it," Bob said. He knelt beside me, stroking my hair from my face. "Let 'em have you, darlin'. Just go with it."

"But that's two--"

"And it's on them. They know what they're dealin' with better'n you do. Enjoy the pleasure and absorb the power. When you transition, I'll be right here with you."

Then he took out his cock and offered me a taste. Unlike the demons, he took it slow. Probably not because he was needing to go at that pace, but because he knew I wasn't ready to come yet. I was proven right when he grinned down at me.

"It's all about timin', baby. They gotta pay attention to you." He pulled his cock away from me and I smiled up at him.

"'Cause I'm the pet."

"And if we don't pay attention to you?"

"I'll destroy things."

Chapter Four

He chuckled. "Exactly. Now. Suck my cock."

He pushed his way back into my mouth while the demons closed in. The two demons inside me were fucking me hard now in a see-saw motion. One in. One out. One out. One in. They grunted and growled. The demon below me played with my tits, the one at my back occasionally swatting my ass. Another ebony demon slid between the two other males and latched on to one of my tits. It wasn't long before there was another on the other side. Bob bared his teeth as he gripped my hair, fucking my mouth with increasing strength.

That feeling of an impending orgasm centered on my clit and I ground myself on the demon I straddled, trying to get friction where I needed it most. My breathing quickened; my body broke out in a sweat. The pressure inside me grew nearly unbearable...

Then I screamed around Bob's cock. He pushed deep, letting go with a long, wet stream of cum inside my mouth. I swallowed frantically, still missing some from the corner of my mouth. The other two demons roared their pleasure, dumping cum inside my pussy and my ass in scorching jets. All around us demons roared and cheered, congratulation their comrades on... not dying?

My own pleasure bordered on cathartic, but inside, I was thrumming like a taut guitar string. Power and energy built inside me, greedily eating up every bit of sexual energy thrown at my body.

I stood on my own, and the demon under me scooted back and three more came forward. Bob leaned in to kiss me just as two of the males picked me up. My back was to one of them. He hooked my legs over his arms to hold my weight and spread me wide. The other guy must have guided him inside my ass because he reached under me, and the next thing I knew a huge cock was forcing its way into my ass. I let my head fall back on the first demon's shoulder while the other one shoved his cock into my pussy.

It took them a moment to get positioned just right, but once they did, they fucked me. Hard.

Mystical energy seemed to swirl around us. I was sure it was the orgasmic high I was on, but it really did look like swirls of plasma-like energy had appeared. But that couldn't be right. Could it?

"Look at her," someone said. Was it just me or were their voices getting more guttural?

"Fuckin' hot little bitch."

"Want my turn next."

"Not if I have anything to say about it." That one came from a big-ass motherfucker. He pushed his way to the front, cock in his fist as he pumped lightly. The thing was huge, red and angry looking. Oh. He was a red demon. I wanted to laugh but was afraid it would come out a strangled cry. Because the longer they worked my body, fucked me hard and wild, the more something build inside me.

It was pleasure, but also a burning heat. Like I was being seared from the inside, burning me clean. I screamed, my body detonating like a bomb. My muscles gripped the cocks inside me, milking them until they spurted deep, the hot cum greedily sucked up by my body.

Immediately, I looked around, searching out my next fuck. I spotted a big, green male making his way forward. Our eyes locked and he nodded once, reaching for me as he stepped forward. He lifted me and immediately sank his dick into my cunt, starting a hard, driving rhythm without any preamble. He wrapped his arms around me, holding me tightly to him, pistoning into me like a jackhammer.

"Fuckin' little whore," he said at my ear. "Fuckin' hot piece." He backed me up against a wall and gripped my hips as he continued to fuck. He looked down into my eyes, baring his teeth. "I may not be able to keep you, but I'm damn sure takin' my fuckin' fill." Pleasure flooded me, the sensations making me come with a scream.

He pulled out of me, roaring and shaking his head as if sheer force of will kept him from coming. "Not yet, beauty. I'm gonna cum deep in your ass," he panted. "But not before I've experienced every fuckin' thing you have to give!"

Setting me on the floor, he shoved me to my knees and gripped my head, shoving his cock in my mouth and down my throat. I squealed around him, throwing my head back to better receive him. He took advantage, sinking himself just that little bit deeper. My throat bulged as he slid all the way down my throat. Again, I swallowed reflexively, massaging him and taking the precum he gave up.

"Ah! Fuck!" He pulled out and gripped my chin hard, leaning down close to my face. "None of that, bitch," he grunted before leaning in to lick my lips. Then he slipped his tongue inside my mouth for a deep kiss. "I'm comin' in deep in that ass." He shook his head. "You ain't takin' my cum before I'm ready."

Then he shoved his dick back inside my mouth, gripping my hair in a tight fist as he fucked my face. Hard. Saliva dripped in a steady stream down my chin. I raised my hands to grip his ass and urge him on. I needn't have bothered. As the pressure built inside me, it seemed to mirror the sensations in him because he growled and snarled, moving harder and faster.

My fingers dug into the muscles of his ass so hard, I was sure I'd left gashes from my fingernails. I could feel his pleasure building. My own wasn't far behind it, but, again, the power was out of balance. I lowered one hand to my clit but he jerked out of my mouth and pulled me to my feet by my hair.

"Now, you fuckin' little bitch, I'm gonna fill your ass full of my cum and you're gonna come when I do."

He turned me to face the wall, then his cock poked at my asshole. Then he was inside me, fucking me hard. Our skin slapped together, loud even over the noise of the demon horde. His snarls at my neck sent shivers through my body. There was no doubt I had a demon at my back.

His hands slid around to my tits, squeezing and milking my nipples as he fucked. All that pleasure and power stayed right on the edge. This demon knew what he was about. He kept me riding the edge as long as he wanted, taking his pleasure but letting it build until we were both ready to explode with the ungodly sensations.

"Now, little succubus," he bit out. "You're gonna come with me now. Fuckin' take me over the edge." His hand was suddenly at my pussy, finding my clit hard and aching with one finger. The second he touched me, I screamed out my pleasure. My ass clenched around his cock, making the fit that much tighter. It burned with the stretch, the opposing sensations warring with each other in the most delicious way.

The demon at my back roared, bucking and grinding his cock deeper as his cum gushed into me. Again, the power flowing through me was indescribable! The aura of plasma swirls around us grew brighter, reds and blacks, along with a stream of white, fighting for dominance.

"So pretty," I whispered as I gazed up at the light spectacle.

"Fucking beautiful." Dokkin stood next to me, but didn't make a move to take his pleasure like Bob had. Instead, he motioned for more of the horde to come for me.

They did. Three more demons. Three more cocks stuffed in every part of me. This time, I was on my back, legs spread by the demon whose chest I lay on. My legs were spread wide in his large hands, his big cock up my ass. Another demon knelt in front of me, shoving his dick in my pussy.

I'd just gotten into it and was working my way toward yet another amazing orgasm when another demon positioned himself in front of the second demon. He gave me a wicked grin and fitted his dick in my pussy alongside the other male's cock.

"There's a good succubus," he purred as he started to work me as hard as the other two. "Starved for demon cock. Demon cum."

"Fill me full of it," I said through the hard pounding my body was taking. "Do it!"

All three of them snarled at me, fucking me hard and fast. It wasn't long before another orgasm threatened, but I couldn't seem to fall over the edge. Frustration built as the demons continued to fuck me with a vicious intensity.

"You better get her there," Mikkos said from somewhere close. I looked around to find all my monsters close. Hovering. Like they were holding vigil or something. None of them other than Bob approached me, though. "She doesn't get off when you do, you'll all three meet the void."

"Fuck! Fuck!" One of the demons -- I had no idea which one -- chanted the mantra as they all continued to fuck me.

Then one squatted down and shoved himself in my mouth. I had no idea if they were just getting carried away or if they just didn't care, but Mikkos, bastard that he was, was right. I was close, but not there yet.

The one on his back, snaked his arm around my body to find my clit between me and the other demon, trying to put some friction on my clit. "Come on, little female," he murmured to me. "They need to come and so do I. Reach for it."

I nodded my head, sweat dripping from my face down my neck to land on his shoulder where I lay. I concentrated on the sensations, closing my eyes and just… feeling.

Someone griped my ass, claws digging into my skin like spurs. It was just enough to send me over the edge into madness. This time, I thrashed and bucked, screaming and screaming until my throat was raw. The guy in my mouth shot his load over my face (smart move!) while the others released into my body as I milked them of their cum. But I didn't stop. I came again. Then again.

And again.

The guy under me gave a strangled shout and I felt his cum spurt inside me yet again. It seemed to trigger another orgasm for me and then one for him. The cycle seemed to not want to break. Especially when another demon took his place over me and started fuck in an almost uncontrollable frenzy. When I came the next time, they both came with me. The demon underneath me thrusting helplessly, his strength waning.

"Get her off me," he gasped. To my surprise, it was Sivvour who lifted me from the pile of demons. "Fuck!" I glanced at the demon on the floor. There was as wisp of white plasma light around him, glowing eerily. One of his companions moved him out of the way before more demons came to take his place.

"How many more?" I gasped. Though, truthfully, I needed more. I could feel it. I wasn't weak. Far from it. I felt like I could run a marathon!

"It's a horde," Sivvour said. "There's fifty-four in total."

Lust hit me like a punch to the gut. I stiffened, squirming until Sivvour put me down. "Fifty-four. I've got a long way to go." I grinned at him over my shoulder then walked into the middle of the remainder of the demon horde.

The pleasure was like nothing else I've ever known or heard of. Unfortunately, more than one of the bastards met the void, as Sivvour called it. And it wasn't because I couldn't come. The more I fucked, the easier it was and I could do it almost at will. Power filled me so much I felt like I was on fire. It was a heady feeling. My strength grew with every orgasm of a demon, every stream of hot cum that found its way inside my body. All the while, the energy swirling around us grew brighter and brighter, the colors all but fading completely until there was only white energy.

"Give her to me!" Bob's voice boomed over the horde's ruckus.

"No!" One of the big demons fucking me snarled. "We're keeping the succubus! She gives us power!"

"Only if you know how to coax it," Bob said, his own temper spiking. I could tell because his fangs lengthened and fur erupted over his body. "You take, you die!"

"As long as she comes, we'll be safe."

"Wanna bet?" I said with a narrowed gaze. I had no idea what possessed me, but I squeezed my pussy. Tight. The demon inside me exploded cum inside me with an almost high-pitched squeal. The second he did, he vanished in a puff of smoke. There was no gradual dissipation, he was just... gone.

Bob grinned. With his fangs and fur it looked as evil as I felt at the moment. "Told you. She's a pet. You don't keep a pet happy, she destroys things."

"I think the female wants to be with us," Dokkin said softly as he approached. "It's time for her transition."

I yelled to the ceiling, energy swirling all around me. "FUCK MEEEE!" I screamed, not knowing what was happening and not really caring. All I knew was that I needed the monsters. My monsters. Right. Fucking. *Now*!

Bob plucked me up from the floor and crossed to a bench. He spread me out on top of him and guided his cock inside me. He was the biggest of any I'd taken today. The biggest of my monsters. But I wanted all of them. Somehow, some way, I needed all five of the bastards. Including Sivvour."

He fucked me, lifting me with each thrust of his hips. "That's it, little female," he purred as he fucked. "Give me what you need. Take what you need."

"Fuck! Your fur is erotic as fuck," I gasped. "*Fuck*!"

Then there was another furry body at my back. Dokkin lay his chin on my shoulder as he guided his cock into my ass. "Gonna enjoy this more than I ever thought possible. You are... exquisite, Wyn. And as lusty a pet as ever there was."

Fukkon appeared at my side. He was still in his more human form, but I could tell he was riding the edge. "Do you have room for me, little succubus?"

I barked out a laugh. "Yeah. Can you manage to get in my ass beside Dokkin?"

He grinned. "Oh yeah." He slid in front of Dokkin and his cock probed my back entrance. It was a stretch, but I took them both.

"I guess that leaves me and Mikkos with your hands," Sivvour muttered.

"Yeah," I retorted, "I guess it does. Just as well, because after the shit you said earlier, you're both lucky I didn't do you like I did the big demon over there."

"Point taken," Mikkos said as he guided my hand to his cock. "Consider that the last time I disparage you, female."

"Same here." Sivvour did the same, both of them guiding me how they wanted me to grip them. Then I cried out, my screams echoing around the room. Every demon there had been fucked senseless. Several of them had passed out toward the end. Not dead or drained, but exhausted. A few from the beginning had recovered enough to help their brothers, but they were all stilled piled in a corner of the room.

As I fucked my monsters, the power around us grew and grew until the light was nearly blinding. I screamed as I came one last time. The monsters roared their pleasure, making the whole place echo with monstrous shouts. I wouldn't be surprised if the valley behind the house was still ringing with the sound. Sivvour was the last to come and he did so in my open mouth, shoving his cock inside and jetting a stream of cum down my throat as I swallowed him over and over.

Then the light exploded all around us. Bob's cock twitched and let loose one last stream of cum inside me. I had to close my eyes, unable to stand the light but having a deep-seated need to embrace it.

One moment it was blinding, the next it was gone, so abruptly we seemed to be in pitch-dark. Several moments passed before I could finally see some shadows. Then everything started to some into focus once more.

My monsters were all around me. Bob still had me on top of him, his arms closed around me, while everyone else either sat or lay on the floor.

"Fuck me raw," Bob grunted. "Fuuuuck."

"Agreed," Dokkin gasped out. "We need to get back to our realm."

"What about the demons?" That was Fukkon. "If we leave them, they'll all meet the void when the sun rises."

Bob chuckled. "If they were stupid enough to help transition a succubus with no way home, they deserve it. Let's go. They either get their asses up or they die. Don't care which."

"For trying to take our prize, they deserve to die," Sivvour said.

"Oh, she's more than a prize," Bob corrected as he stood with me. I didn't miss the fact he was a little unsteady on his feet. "She's our mate."

"Agreed." Dokkin gave his opinion immediately. "Now, let's get her home."

I have no idea how they managed it, but the next thing I knew I was in a hot shower with all of them around me, soaping me from head to toe. If there was more than one licking and sucking me, I didn't complain.

"Do I have to worry 'bout not coming before you now?" I was so sleepy my words were slurring. Now that the power and orgasmic highs were wearing off, I was crashing hard.

"Nah," Bob said as he kissed my mouth gently. "We have to worry about making you come before us. All part of keeping the little woman happy."

I chuckled. "Fine. But if I accidentally kill one of you, don't blame me."

"No," Fukkon said. "That would be all on us."

They stopped the shower and dried me off. Dokkin carried me to that big bed where this adventure had all begun. When he laid me down, I looked up into his eyes. "Do I have to go back to my world now?"

"No, Wyn," he said, brushing back a lock of my hair. "You're here with us now."

"Forever?"

He quirked an eyebrow. "Or until you kill us."

"Try not to let that happen," I said, sniffing indignantly. "I'd hate to have to explain to Daemon why I came back to them. Not sure they'd want me back."

"Probably not," Fukkon said with a soft chuckle. "You're way more woman than any of those pussies can handle."

I sighed happily. "Good. Now. I need sleep. Don't be gone when I wake."

"Wild demons couldn't drag us away."

I had no idea who said that last, because I passed out -- dreaming of the monsters in my closet.

Wanda Violet O.

Welcome to Wanda Violet O.'s world of bedtime fantasy, where you'll find a variety of sexy creatures ready to drink their fill. Wanda specializes in extreme kink. Monsters, BDSM, Role Play... she's got it all. Come take a look for yourself!

Wanda at Changeling: changelingpress.com/wanda-violet-o-a-226

Changeling Press LLC

Contemporary Action Adventure, Sci-Fi, Steampunk, Dark Fantasy, Urban Fantasy, Paranormal, and BDSM Romance available in e-book, audio, and print format at ChangelingPress.com – MC Romance, Werewolves, Vampires, Dragons, Shapeshifters and Horror -- Tales from the edge of your imagination.

Where can I get Changeling Press Books?

Changeling Press e-books are available at ChangelingPress.com, Amazon, Apple Books, Barnes & Noble, Kobo, Smashwords, and other online retailers, including Everand Subscription and Kobo Subscription Services. Print books are available at Amazon, Barnes and Noble, and by ISBN special order through your local bookstores.

Razor's Edge Press
A Changeling Press LLC Imprint

Made in the USA
Columbia, SC
29 June 2024

37836465R00075